As a person who has traveled to Havana, Cuba, on three occasions, I am anticipating reading Christmas in Havana. Having spent a number of days there, I know that the city is filled with history, mystery, and intrigue. Stephen Hiemstra has the ability to capture this mystery and intrigue and much more! Read the book and see what I mean!

Percy M. Burns
Author of *Glorious Freedom*

This book represents a fascinating story that leads to reflection, an adventure of emotions that reflect life itself. in which we can see ourselves reflected at some point after this. Stephen Hiemstra guides us in a very enjoyable way through this book to value life.

Julio Martinez
Senior Pastor
Shadai Phoenix Church

New beginnings for Phil Stevens and Yong Dae Chû as they accept the past merged with new identities. Pastor Phil, is Luke, an agent with the CIA working to defeat the terrorists who killed his son. Beautiful North Korean, Yong Dae Chû, is Ruth, a law student and model. The final book of a three-book series, Christmas in Havana, by Stephen Hiemstra, concludes the story of loss, grief, and self-forgiveness against the backdrop of international terrorism and human trafficking. It is a fast-moving drama filled with action and romance, grounded in spiritual truth.

Sharron Giambanco
Business owner and writer

CHRISTMAS
IN HAVANA

Other Books by the Author

Christian Spirituality Series:
A Christian Guide to Spirituality
Life in Tension
Called Along the Way
Simple Faith
Living in Christ
Image and Illumination

Image of God series:
Image of God in the Parables
Image of the Holy Spirit and the Church

Masquerade series:
Masquerade
The Detour
Christmas in Havana

Translations:
Una Guía Cristiana a la Espiritualidad
Vida en Tensión
Ein Christlicher Leitfaden zur Spiritualität
Oraciones

Prayerbooks:
Everyday Prayers for Everyday People
Prayers
Prayers of a Life in Tension

Screenplays:
Brandishing the Blue
The Korean Detour
Christmas in Havana

CHRISTMAS IN HAVANA

Stephen W. Hiemstra

T2PNEUMA PUBLISHERS LLC
CENTREVILLE, VIRGINIA

Christmas in Havana

 ISNI: 0000-0000-2902-8171

Names: Hiemstra, Stephen W., author.
Title: Christmas in Havana / Stephen W. Hiemstra.
Series: Masquerade Series.
Description: Centreville, VA: T2Pneuma Publishers LLC, 2024.
Identifiers: LCCN: 2024902254 | ISBN: 978-1-942199-47-2 (paperback) | 978-1-942199-94-6 (KDP) | 978-1-942199-85-4 (epub)
Subjects: LCSH United States. Central Intelligence Agency--Officials and employees--Fiction. | Intelligence officers--United States--Fiction. | Law students--Fiction. | Korean-Americans--Fiction. | Cuba--Fiction. | Romantic suspense fiction. | BISAC FICTION / General | FICTION / Romance / Suspense
Classification: LCC PS3608.I328 C47 2024 | DDC 813.6--dc23

Many thanks to my editors, Sarah Hamaker and Jean Arnold.

The cover art is called *Esther's Gamble* by He Qi (www.heqiart.com). Used with permission.

ACT ONE

Chapter 1

Luke Stevens stared into his fireplace with the radio playing in background. The yellow flames danced around the newsprint that he pushed under the split wood. Hot fingers reminded him to pull his hand back, which he does with koala-bear urgency. *Why did Sarah talk so much about collecting firewood and so seldom actually burned it? Even on a Saturday night in January, McLean, Virginia is seldom cold. Who leads such a leisurely life that they can light a fire and sit long enough to watch it?*

A radio news reporter broke into the set. "This just in. A Taiwanese freighter, the New Moon, navigating the waters off the Columbian coast burst into flames without warning and sank with all hands on board. We will keep you informed of any further developments." The radio returned to its usual set, offering jazz from the 1930s.

Luke starred at the radio, not processing what was just reported. His cell phone buzzed and he picked it up.

"Hello, Alex?"

"Luke, how are you doing? Are you ready for the memorial service tomorrow?"

Luke poked the fire with the iron, tossed another piece of wood on top, and glanced at the three-by-five-foot portrait of the former Sarah Stevens, then Sarah Gomer, leaning against the wall.

"I toyed with the idea of torching the house for insurance money, buying an RV, and taking off for Alaska. Instead, I lit the fireplace and decided to pretend that I did."

"Good choice. Are you sure you are ready for this service?" Alex Sunday spoke with the authority of a counselor, a surgeon, and a major in the U.S. Marines, all of which she was.

"I'm sure that I'm not, but the guests have been invited, the eulogy is written, and, now, I'm steeling myself to say goodbye, this time for keeps—Sarah has haunted me long enough."

"How can I help?"

"You mean, outside of wearing your dress blues,

bringing your family, and watching my dad?"

"You know what I mean."

"Yes... Yes, I do. It's enough for you to be there."

"What happens if *she* shows up? Are ready to face her?"

"No. That's why you are going to wear your sword."

"Ha. Ha. Get serious."

"If RJ—Miss Randy Jefferson—shows up, I'll invite her to sit up front with the family. Everyone knows that she is the former Miss Teen USA. What else can I do? I'm still a pastor and have to model forgiveness, painful as it might be. Why couldn't Sarah have just found a nice NFL player, Arab prince, or real estate mogul?"

"It sounds like you have some unresolved issues that I suspect will not make it into the eulogy."

"That's an understatement. Sarah cut herself off from me in the divorce, but the shame also isolated her from her family. Christians are quicker than Muslims to forgive, especially in the case of unconventional relationships. In an honor-shame culture, the path to reconciliation is very nonlinear because difficult and shameful topics are handled with a deafening silence."

"Who will attend the memorial service?"

"Good question. I called her office; I informed her family. Only members of the church, which she disavowed when we divorced, are likely to show up and they may only come out of respect for their grieving pastor."

"Why is it so hard for you to let go?"

"I failed as a husband and as a witness."

"None of us is perfect or a perfect witness."

"My head accepts what my heart rejects."

"Then on faith you must give it over to God—especially if you hope to love again."

Chapter 2

Yong Dae Chŭ—Ruth—leaned against the ivy-covered library at her law school in Washington D.C. She held her arm unnaturally high in a pose wearing a red knit cap and scarf, and a white sweater.

"Hold up that law journal." The photographer from a Korean fashion magazine instructed her.

Ruth grabed a journal from a leather bag setting on a nearby step. She righted herself, held the journal near her face, and smiled.

"Seems odd to me that Americanized Koreans only want the fashion photos, while folks back home want to hear that I'm also editor of my school law journal."

"It's a head scratcher for sure," The photographer replied. "But we both know it's a real thing—the magazine will print both. The only unsettled question is which photo will make the cover."

"An American audience would prefer to see me holding a Russian Blue or playing with a French Bulldog."

"For sure."

"Be sure to mention that the feature article in the law journal this month is about artificial intelligence (AI). AI is a hot topic, not only in law, but in business and military procurement. My editorial has already received several reprint offers in commercial publications."

"You are too smart. How will you ever find an American husband, assuming you want one? American men find smart women intimidating."

"You are too mean. Why do you think I agreed to this photo shoot?"

"You are killing me—I assumed that it was just because you wanted to see me again."

"That too! But you know fashion helps a single girl live into her feminine mystique."

"Right. All work and no play makes Jack a dull boy, kind of thing, to quote James Howell."

"People forget the simplest things." Ruth turned to the photographer and put on a serious face. "Let me ask a more difficult question: Is the magazine planning to write about my escape from North Korea into China last fall and the human trafficking issue?

"I like how you are always straight to the point." The photographer relaxed, lowering the camera from his view. "The editor told me that political topics are normally off-point in a fashion magazine and won't be cited in your article."

He paused, then continued. "Because you have become the poster-child of the North Korean immigrant issue in the Korean press, every time people see your face, they think about the suffering of North Korean women in China sold into brothels and marriages with leftover men. If they forget, the next article after yours will focus on the problem of repatriation of North Koreans caught in China, but it does not mention you by name."

"Oh, good. I feel so much more desirable. In any case, thanks for being honest and letting me know."

§

As Ruth walked back to her dorm, she noticed a short, thin man with crew cut, black tie, and green-tan suit standing with a woman dressed in a matching suit-skirt combination across the street and watching her. She laughed as they crossed the street and came up to her.

"What are you laughing about?" asked the woman.

"I'm going to recommend a new fashion consultant to Director Parks the next time I see him." Ruth replied.

"Not funny. We're here on business," The man said.

"Oh, what business? Are you lost in the 1950s?"

"Ha. Ha. Director Parks sent us to remind you of your debt to the Reconnaissance General Bureau (RGB)."

"Haven't you heard? I'm an American student now, not a visiting scholar from Kim Il-sung University. I have even been given a green card."

"Your family remains our guests in Najin."

"I understand. I hope that means you will issue my family extra rations and my mother a cell phone so that I can call her."

"You are most greedy."

"Not at all. Everyone here has a cell phone and can buy whatever they can afford. Why are North Koreans any less worthy than Americans to enjoy their lives? Come back to me when you have my mom's number."

"Director Parks will not be pleased."

"You misunderstand Director Parks. He is a decent man in an indecent time. He will thank God that I have given him the opportunity to undertake an ounce of charity while a pound of uncharitable duties disgusts him. I respect Director Parks and wish him well."

"You will hear from us."

"You know my name. Who are you?"

"Goodbye, Ms. Chǔ."

Chapter 3

At their home in McLean Virginia, Natalie heard her mother knock on her bedroom door: "May I come in?"

"The door is open."

Natalie turned from her desk chair to watch her mother walk in. She moved some of the books piled up on the desk and placed them on the floor. Turning back to her laptop computer, she saved a half-completed essay and closed the closed the lid to give full attention to her mom.

"Working again? Classes don't start for a couple weeks. You need to give yourself a break."

"Mom. I get bored just sitting around on my days off from work. The high school gang seem stuck in the past. I would much rather read my class assignments, write my essays, and get ready for the term."

"I understand, but tonight you need to get ready for the memorial service tomorrow after church. Pastor Luke is single and you don't want to be forever."

"Pastor Luke has morphed into his father, Phil. Luke was fun; now, he has become all serious like his dad. I preferred the old Luke."

"Perhaps, but he is still single, available, and decent. Old fashioned, decent men are hard to come by these days."

"Okay. You have made your point. I think if I were Muslim that you would still send me to church on Sundays." Natalie turned off her surge-protector and tidied up her desk. "Could you help me with my hair? I need a trim."

"Sure, dear. I love your long, blond hair."

Chapter 4

Still sensitive about being seen in the company of other Christians, Ruth organized a small gathering of Korean students on campus for worship on Sunday morning. She arranged for local Korean congregations to support the group with a rotating schedule of visiting pastors that helped them remain accountable to one another and advance their knowledge of scripture. She suggested that the cafeteria outsource Sunday lunch by contracting for a local Korean restaurant to cater the meal, which gave the cafeteria workers a bit more time off and boosted attendance at the luncheon. Ruth thought of this group as a house church, but they simply called themselves the Korean Alliance.

After lunch, Ruth returned to her dorm room, slipped into a black dress with matching shoes, white sweater, knit cap, and scarf. She brushed her teeth, put on some bright-red lipstick, and arranged for a car to drive her to Luke's church in McLean for the two p.m. memorial service.

As Ruth got into the car, she handed the driver the address of the church. "Can you take Canal Road up to Chain Bridge?"

"No problem," the driver responded. "Actually, it's the most direct route."

"I love to watch the river flowing over the rocks and to take in the relaxing scenery of the park."

Traffic on Canal Road proved to be light. The Potomac River raged with winter thaw from up in the Allegany Mountains. Still, Ruth could see afternoon hikers along the canal occasionally through the woods. Once across the bridge, it was all metes and bounds—Old Glebe, Chesterbrook, Kirby, and Great Falls Roads. Charming, scenic, relaxing.

As the car pulled up to the rear entrance to the church, Ruth asked the driver, "This is the church? It's so big."

"This is a medium-sized church. There is a much bigger church a couple miles across town. It's like an indoor shopping mall with confession stands, breakout rooms the size of normal church sanctuaries, and its own gymnasium, just for kids," the driver said.

"Are you sure this is the right church?"

"Yes. This is the address that you provided."

Ruth opened the car door. "Thanks." Nervous. She got out, closed the door behind her, and walked up the steps into building.

§

Once inside, two little girls, ages five or six, ran past her and down a staircase. Ruth could do nothing more than simply stop and watch.

"Maria, Pilar—donde están?" Ruth heard from down the hall.

The two girls looked up and giggled from down the stairs and ran off.

A teenage girl hurried down the hall towards Ruth. "Have you seen a couple of kids running around?"

Ruth lifted her hand to point. "They ran down the stairs."

"Thanks," responded the teenager as she hurried down the steps.

"Do you know where to find the memorial service for Sarah Gomer?" Ruth asked.

The teen stopped and looked back. "Keep going down the hall and around the corner to the left. Then just follow the crowd into the narthex."

§

Ruth wandered down the hall to where she heard people conversing as they walked up a small set of stairs into a narthex. Before she got there, Maria and her friend, Pilar, ran up another staircase into the narthex and threw their arms around Tom Roberts, the first person that Ruth recognized—the CIA agent in charge who helped her leave China and get settled in the United States.

"Tom, so good to see you again. I see that you are quite the ladies' man."

"Ruth. I wondered if you would show up today. How is school?"

"It's good to be out of the limelight and back to studying law. Have you seen Luke?"

"He is up front in the sanctuary. The service is

about to begin, so perhaps you can catch him afterwards at the reception downstairs in fellowship hall."

"Of course. Do you mind if I sit with you during the service?"

"No problem. Let's go in."

§

Ruth entered the sanctuary with Tom and the two girls as the organ prelude began playing *Softly and Tenderly Jesus is Calling*. The packed church forced them to sit in the back pew with the two girls between them giggling and squirming. In a vain hope to settle the girls down, Ruth offered them some peppermints that she kept in her purse. Looking ahead, Ruth could barely see the portrait of Sarah standing up on an easel because of the people sitting in front of them.

Ruth leaned over the girls to whisper to Tom. "How come Sarah is having a Christian service? Wasn't she Muslim?"

"Yes, she was, but because Luke and his father, Phil, both pastored at this church for most of her marriage, Sarah served as pastor's wife here in this church.

Everyone remembers her, and there is a family plot out in the graveyard behind the church."

"So her relationship with this church was solid, but complicated?"

"That's a good interpretation. Things got even more complicated when Sarah left Phil to live with a woman, Randy Johnson."

Ruth flinched when she heard about Sarah leaving Phil. *Oh my,* she thought. *No wonder Luke was knotted up about bringing Sarah back from Beijing and losing her when their plane crashed in the Korean East Sea.* As Ruth wiped a few tears away, she noticed that Alex Sunday came in with an old man and forced a smile at her. They both wore colorful uniforms and sat in folding chairs immediately behind her.

§

The music stopped. Ruth saw Pastor Elizabeth Robbins step up in front of the communion table dressed in a creme-colored robe with a black stole. Her eyes surveyed the congregation very deliberatively.

"Friends in Christ, today we're here to honor the

memory of Sarah Gomer, whom many of us remember as Sarah Stevens. Sarah passed away this past month during a visit to Beijing, China, as a result of an aggressive case of ovarian cancer. Her remains were later lost in the Sea of Japan in a typhoon plane crash that claimed the lives of numerous passengers. Thankfully, dear Pastor Luke, who was also on the flight, survived the crash and was rescued by a North Korean fishing boat. He will now share a few words about his mom."

Pastor Elizabeth extended her arm towards Luke, and took a seat behind the reader's pulpit on the right side of the sanctuary.

Ruth watched as Luke stepped into the preaching pulpit on the left side of the sanctuary. His face appeared as if he had been crying. "Thank you, Elizabeth. You have been a great comfort to the family in the midst of these trying times."

An old man in Navy whites stood up behind Ruth and shouted: "Phil—You can't fool me. You are the only one who comes to visit me. You are not Luke. Luke died in a shootout with terrorists in Baltimore."

Alex hustled Commander Stevens out of the sanctuary and into the Narthex.

Ruth gasped with her hand over her mouth. She thought, *Phil wasn't even in Baltimore, and he assumed his son, Luke's, identity.*

Pastor Elizabeth Robbins stood up again, "Please excuse Commander Stevens. For those of you unaware, he suffers from Alzheimer's Disease and as a retired naval officer, normally resides in the memory care unit on Kirby Road." She turned to Luke looking so as to say—*I'm so sorry…go on*—and sat down.

Flustered, Luke mumbled a few words about Sarah's life and sat down. Ruth noticed a young woman with beautiful long, blond hair sitting up front following Luke's every word, every move, however awkward, *You are not the only one who looks on Luke with soft eyes.* Ruth thought.

Pastor Elizabeth stood up again. "Would anyone else like to share a memory of Sarah?"

Ruth noticed that Elizabeth's eyes seemed to float around until they came to rest on an attractive black woman sitting off to the side. The woman averted her eyes, disdaining the invitation. *Who is that woman?* She thought.

Not a peep could be heard.

Elizabeth scrutinized the room. She then offered a prayer for Sarah and dismissed the congregation with a blessing.

Chapter 5

Ruth followed Tom and the girls down the steps to the fellowship hall reception. She was searching faces for Alex when she ran into the young blond, who held out her hand.

"Hi. My name is Natalie. How do you know Sarah?"

"Good to meet you, Natalie. I'm Ruth. Sarah and I were not acquainted; we never even met."

"Then you must know Luke. How did you meet?"

"Luke and I traveled together in Korea last fall after his plane crash."

"Oh, you are *that* Ruth. I saw one of your interviews on television. You are too modest—you smuggled Luke out of North Korea against all odds in the middle of the night. So are you two dating?"

"No. Dating is out of the question. My mother would like me to find a nice Korean boy. Luke and I haven't seen each other since my uncle's church reception after we arrived in the United States. How do you know Luke?"

"We live in the same neighborhood, and my family attends this church."

"Luke is your pastor?"

"Yes. My mother has been after me to go out with him."

"Who was that the attractive black woman that Pastor Elizabeth was prodding in the service?"

"That was the former Miss Teenage USA, Randy Jefferson. Sarah divorced Luke's father, Phil, to move in with her, which is probably why Pastor Elizabeth was encouraging her to speak."

"Poor ... Luke." Ruth said stumbling over the words, wishing she could rephrase her comment. "He lost both of his parents this fall."

Natalie just smiled at her.

§

Ruth winced at Natalie and continued searching for Alex, slowly wandering around fellowship hall and avoiding the desert table. Lost and lonely in the crowd, she caught a glimpse of a light-green suit coat and a man who looked like Lei Han, but she felt light-headed and convinced herself that she was just hallucinating—*Why did I ever leave my family in Korea to come to the United States?* Then she noticed Commander Stevens sitting in a chair against the wall while Alex helped him eat a piece of cake without soiling his dress-whites. She walked over and sat next to Alex.

"Alex. It's good to see you again," Ruth began.

"Back at you, girl. Have a seat. How is school?"

"School is great. American students have it so easy. My scholarship pays all my expenses, so I have a private dorm room, plenty to eat, and money for books."

"I hear that you are doing some modeling on the side. Is that true?"

"Guilty as charged. My agent arranged for me to get a credit card and takes me on shopping trips to pick out fashionable clothes."

"Neat. I used to model for *Ebony* magazine, but they were never that generous."

"I'm sorry." Ruth suddenly looked distracted

and aloof. "Alex, tell me about Commander Steven's little outburst. What was that about?"

"Commander Steven's Alzheimer's affliction leaves him disoriented at times. You never know what he will do or say."

"His comment was rather pointed. Why did he confuse Luke with his father?"

"Phil Stevens lost a lot of weight after Sarah divorced him so much so that Luke and Phil could wear the same clothes. A lot of people confused them, not just Commander Stevens."

"Oh. Phil must have really loved her."

"Seriously."

§

As Ruth was talking with Alex, Luke walked up with a couple of paper plates with cake and forks.

"Is anyone hungry?" Luke handed Ruth a paper plate and sat down. Ruth looked up and her radiant green eyes twinkled when their eyes met.

"Now that you mention it—I was eyeing that cake."

"This cake is special; I picked it out myself. The baker specializes in wedding cakes using old-fashioned pound-cake recipes that are hard to find in this age of ice-cream cake and low-calorie, pseudo-cake deserts. I hope that you approve."

"Absolutely. You are a man after my own heart. My hobby back at home in school was baking. Actually, I had a small catering service side-hustle."

"Is that right?"

"No. I'm lying—cake ingredients back home were nearly impossible to obtain at any price. The main staple in most kitchens was low-quality corn meal. Wheat products, as well as sugar and refined flour, were luxury items."

"Well perhaps you should re-evaluate your side-hustle now that the ingredients are readily available." Luke set his paper plate down on a chair without having touched the cake. "Ruth, can I ask you a personal question?"

"Sure, what's up?"

"I'm organizing a *Mardi Gras* (fat-Tuesday) party next month at church to draw people's attention to the beginning of Lent. I was wondering if you would join me as my guest? I know it's a school night, but I would be happy to come pick you up and bring you home. What do you say?"

"What day is that?"

"Tuesday, February 13th."

"Okay. Give me your cell-phone number so we can hammer out details later that week."

"Super."

Ruth's mind raced with excitement, but she almost immediately regretted getting caught up in the moment. *How can my relationship with Luke go anywhere? How can I be honest with him? What would Director Parks say?*

"Ruth, so you know—this party is something of a going-away event for me. My office is sending me to the FBI Academy at Quantico Marine Base for three months of training starting the first week in March.

"Oooh. Sounds like fun!"

ACT TWO

Chapter 6

Monday morning, Ruth got up and skipped breakfast to go for a run. The cold January wind blew across campus and whistled through the newly shattered street light in front of her dorm. In a place like DC, one does not want to walk in the dark at night. Normally, the campus maintenance staff would be right on it, but two days had passed since the shattering, and it had become a topic of conversation among the women in her dorm. Ruth tired of the old argument comparing and contrasting the advantages of pepper spray versus packing heat. *Isn't it enough to have a black belt in karate?* She told herself as she returned to the dorm. *American women are too lazy.*

Ruth labored to stay focused as she showered and got dressed. *How can I understand Chinese law, human rights, and accounting with my mind on Mardi Gras? If that weren't bad enough, the law journal committee needs proofs edited by Wednesday. Why again did I volunteer to edit?*

Walking to class, Ruth ruminated on what costume to wear for the party. What do Americans really wear for *Mardi Gras*? Her first class at eight o'clock was just a block from her dorm, but as she sat at her desk, pulled out her notebook, and looked up to see the professor she could not remember the walk over. *OMG. Am I even in the right building?* Fortunately, all was in order, except that she sat down next to a creepy guy whom she swore to herself that she would avoid. *Oh well, it's only for an hour, and he seemed to have bathed this week.*

§

Walking out of her dorm after lunch, Ruth found her two light-green-suited friends waiting for her.

"Director Parks approved your request. Your family will receive additional food rations and your mother has a new cell phone. Cell service is limited to Sundays from noon to four o'clock local time in Najin." The man handed Ruth an index card with a telephone number written on it. "Don't let us down."

"Your names?"

"Have a nice day, Ms. Chǔ. We will be in touch,"

the man said. He and the woman walked off.

Chapter 7

Tom received a text from Alex late in the morning asking for a meeting in person. Tom picked up the phone and called her.

"Hello, Alex. Would you like to get together for a late lunch, say one p.m.?"

"That works. Where?"

"I'll send a car to pick you up at twelve-thirty."

"Got it."

Alex and Tom got together in a quiet steak restaurant in McLean.

Having ordered, Tom asked, "Alex, what's on your mind?"

"Yesterday at Sarah's memorial service, I'm sure I saw Lei Han masquerading as a North Korean intelligence officer. He was pretty hard to miss in his light-green suit. What was weird is that although he disguised his appearance, it seemed that he wanted me to see him," Alex said.

"I saw him, too. I think you are right, but why?"

"I have no idea. Abi Ling is out of the picture, and the last time that I heard Lei Han was under arrest in China. Why would he come back to the United States and risk arrest?"

"It may be a bit of bravado. Before I left Beijing last month, Harry Bai warned me that several impolitic actions by the current U.S. administration —things that in Washington we might call boneheaded or describe as in-your-face lame—were strengthening the hand of hardliners in the Chinese government. Even Abi's father, the Premier, was on the defensive and forced to take a harder line," Tom said.

"What does it mean?"

"Unclear. Harry said that he hand-picked Abi's security team because he worried that she would become a person of interest and be forced to seek asylum."

"That's a pretty radical concern for the Minister of State Security, wouldn't you say?"

"For sure. I'm not sure, however, what any of this has to do with Lei Han and his fascination with

Abi."

"That's a real head scratcher. Is Lei Han being tracked?"

"Yes, ever since the reception. It's as though he wanted us to track him."

§

Around four p.m., Tom stopped by Luke's office at CIA Headquarters in Langley, Virginia.

"Knock, knock," he said.

"Come in, Tom. Thanks for attending Sarah's memorial service yesterday. Your daughter is adorable."

"I wouldn't have missed it. How are you doing?"

"I'm ready to reboot my life and move on, although it may take a while."

"That's totally expected. How are your preparations coming for the FBI Academy in March?"

"I'm training morning and evening six days a week under the supervision of the office physical therapist. She says that I should be ready to pass the physical screening test in mid-February. Meanwhile, I'm spending my days going through the required reading so that I'll come across in class like a Navy Seal taking in a refresher course."

"Good. It must be difficult masquerading as a younger man with a military background."

"I did think of a question that you might be able to help me with. What was my son's handle in the Seals? Someone at Quantico is bound to ask me about that."

"You don't know? They called him *pastor*."

"Luke's handle was *pastor*?"

"Yep. Pastor. Now that you mentioned it, I'm going to pass you your son's personnel file so you don't get outed by some detail from his background. At Quantico, you are likely to meet people who served with him."

"Thanks."

Luke pauses.

"Tom, can I change the subject for a minute?"

"Sure. What's up?"

"I have asked Ruth to go with me to a *Mardi Gras* celebration next week at church. Is that going to be a problem?"

"Your personal life is yours to manage. Keep in mind, however, that none of us can talk about our work outside the office, and everyone we associate with is, of course, subject to periodic review."

"Right. I remember the briefing on security."

"I should share one thing with you about the memorial service."

"What's that?" Luke looked puzzled.

"Several of us observed Lei Han walking around yesterday at your reception."

"What? I thought Lei Han was arrested in China."

"He was, but the Chinese situation is volatile at the moment with hardliners gaining the upper hand. Abi's father, the Premier, is still in office, but he has been forced to alter his political positions and he may be a short-timer."

"Oh, my goodness. I hope that Abi is okay."

"Abi is back to studying medicine in Baltimore."

"Thanks for letting me know—I wondered why she ducked the memorial service."

"I'm sure that she is just keeping a low profile. It's nice that Abi and Sarah got along so well in Beijing."

"Yes."

Chapter 8

Ruth called her mother at eleven o'clock the following Saturday evening from McLean, which was noon on Sunday in Najin, North Korea.

"Mom?" Ruth said.

"Yes, dear."

"How are you?"

"I'm suffering miserably. Your father was lost at sea. The Tsushima current carried his boat north and east to be deposited on the Shakotan Peninsula along the Japanese coast. The hull was riddled with bullet holes and the boat stripped of its engine. His body was never found."

"When did this happen?"

"We don't know exactly, but he never returned from the trip the night that you left. What happened to you?"

"I escaped into China with Mr. Stevens and was given asylum in the United States. I'm now a law student in Washington, D.C. Now and then I see Uncle Chŭ, father's older half-brother who is a pastor near me in Virginia."

"Director Parks' people came by last week. We're receiving better rations now, and they gave us this phone. What did he ask from you?

"Director Parks has asked nothing of me as yet, but I owe him for these favors."

"Be careful, dear."

Ruth talked with each member of the family who were present. At three a.m. Sunday morning, the line went dead and she went to bed. Almost immediately thereafter, she received a text from a North Korea area code for Pyongyang.

Director Parks: *Please give Tom this number (850-381-xxxx) the next time you see him.*

Excited and perplexed, Ruth tried to sleep but tossed and turned all night.

§

In the morning around seven o'clock, Ruth called Luke.

"Good morning, Luke. How are you?"

"I'm good. I was just getting ready to go for a

run. What's up?"

"I promised to call you to work out details for *Mardi Gras,* and I wanted to catch you before work."

"What's on your mind?"

"What time do I need to be ready, and what should I wear?"

"The party starts at eight o'clock, so I should pick you up around seven on Tuesday. You can wear anything you like—presumably a costume, but be sure to include a mask."

"Great. I can do that. My fashion agent will love this event. Do you mind if I invite his photographer?

"No problem. I'm always curious what to expect from my fashion-model-in-residence friend. I can't imagine how you manage to be a full-time law student on top of everything you do."

"I have a lot of energy. Actually, it's hard to sit still in lengthy classes. Have you invited Alex and Tom?"

"As a matter of fact, I did tell them about it."

"I would feel funny attending a party where I

don't know anyone. Listen, I have to run to class. See you Tuesday."

"Bye. Thanks for calling."

Ruth texted Director Parks.

Ruth: *I hope to pass your greetings to Tom on Tuesday evening, February 13th, at a social event. Is that sufficiently prompt?*

Director Parks: *Yes.*

§

Ruth's agent took her shopping over the next weekend to pick out a costume for *Mardi Gras*. After much discussion, they found a long golden-yellow silk robe with matching gray shawl and hat, and a white mask designed to resemble Queen Esther's attire, perfect for a cold evening in February. In spite of the fun outing, she worried about whether Tom would show up at the party and, if he did, what she would tell him about her role as a RGB courier. She truly felt like Queen Esther contemplating approaching the King unannounced.

Chapter 9

Luke hung up after speaking with Ruth. Already dressed to run, he grabbed a knit cap, put on a pair of gloves, and headed for the door. As he turned the door knob, he stopped, took off the gloves, picked up his cell phone, and dialed Tom's cell phone.

"Hello, Luke?"

"Tom, sorry to bother you so early. I just got off the phone with Ruth. Are you doing anything Tuesday evening next week? Would you like to join us for my *Mardi Gras* celebration?"

"Sure. No problem. What brought this on? You seem to have something on your mind."

"Well, yes. This was Ruth's idea. I'm not sure why. Actually, she asked about Alex coming as well."

"Obviously, it's because we're a tight-knit group. We work and play together on multiple continents. I'll pass on your invite to Alex."

"Thanks, Tom. Bring your daughter, if you like. Anyhow, I'm going for my run."

Chapter 10

Tuesday evening, Ruth saw Luke drive up in front of her dorm building dressed like a priest with a black suit, shirt, and mask topped with a clerical collar. Except for the mask, he did not look out of place in the Roman Catholic University. When he came up to her dorm, Ruth could not believe the look on his face when she opened the door and he saw her costume. There he stood, wide-eyed, and mouth gaping.

"Hey Father, come right in," Ruth said.

"I think that I know now why you invited a photographer to meet us at the church," Luke responded.

"I try not to disappoint. Whom do I look like?"

"You look too good to be anyone I know."

"But whom do I look like?"

"Perhaps an Arab princess."

"Now you are getting it. I'm supposed to be Queen Esther."

"I was going to say Esther. You will make the rest of us look plain and unimaginative."

"Right."

"Are you ready?"

"Let's go. Can you drive to the church by way of Canal Road? I would like to take in the river in the moonlight."

"You are an undying romantic."

§

When Ruth and Luke arrived at the church, people were waiting on the steps and in their cars decked out in elaborate costumes. If Lent is an austere forty days before Easter when the faithful study, pray, and fast, *Mardi Gras* is a foretaste of the Marriage Feast of the Lamb—a chance to kick back, celebrate, and get a little crazy. After years of pandemic and worry about the end times and violence, the church displayed its ongoing readiness to consider an alternative future.

Luke jumped out of his car, ran up to the door, and let people in. Meanwhile, Ruth's photographer coached her on exiting from the car and posing on the steps of the church, roping in party-goers with costumes fitting the occasion to highlight the scenes. The photographer took special interest in Tom who dressed as a Knight Templar with a little lady-in-waiting at his side—his daughter.

After having her picture taken, Ruth said. "Tom, I'm glad to see you. Director Parks texted me last week and asked me to give you his number." Ruth handed Tom an index card with the number.

"Did he indicate a reason to call?"

"No. I asked him if this request was urgent, but he said no."

"Okay. I'll give him a call."

§

Inside the church, Luke ran ahead to kick things off, leaving Ruth and her photographer to take a few more shots in the sanctuary. Once they finished up there, the photographer suggested that they take a few more photographs, this time during the party. Previously distracted, Ruth now noticed the *Mardi Gras* celebration from the strobe lights and music coming out of the fellowship hall down a staircase from the sanctuary. She makes her way down the stairs careful not to trip over her costume.

"Hey, stranger. Love your costume!" Natalie said, standing at the door to fellowship hall dressed like Little Bo Peep with a white bonnet, blue checkered dress with white sleeves and gloves, and a shepherd's cane.

"Wow. You are gorgeous," Ruth responded.

"Why thank you," Natalie said with a bow. "Can I ask you a personal question?"

"Why not?"

"I thought you were looking for a nice Korean boy," Natalie said. "How come I keep seeing you in the company of Pastor Luke?

"You're not supposed to notice that."

"Why not?"

"I'm new to this idea of open dating. Back home, men and women don't date—they scheme through common acquaintances and relatives to show up at public events together. Or they just end up in arranged marriages."

"Sounds complicated."

"Really," Ruth agreed. "How about you? Why

haven't you found someone?"

"It's hard. I'm nineteen and just graduated from college. Guys my age seem immature, and my classmates are usually intimidated by smart and attractive women. My mother complains that I study too much, but it's because I'm bored."

"Wow. I took you for a high school student."

"You and everyone else."

"What are you going to do?"

"Right now, I work and take graduate school classes to keep my mind busy."

§

While Ruth was busy with Natalie, Luke went into fellowship hall and found Alex sitting by herself, dressed like a sailor in dress whites. The contrast with her dark complexion gave her a youthful look, but she appeared out of sorts. Luke walked over and sat next to her.

"What's up, Alex? You seem distracted."

"I'm not a party person. I'm more private; I enjoy my peace and space."

"We're on the same wave length."

"You seemed flustered at the memorial service. Have you found your peace with Sarah?"

"The service was challenging, but I took your advice to give my pain over to God. Grief comes and goes, but it no longer defines my days."

"Good to hear. Enough of my pestering. Go enjoy yourself with Ruth."

Chapter 11

Wednesday morning, Tom requested clearance to call Director Parks on a secure telephone line that could record the conversation. His curiosity about the call was palpable because the absence of official contact with the RGB had led to many unfortunate incidents. He decided that the best time to call would be that afternoon at five, which would be six in the morning in Pyongyang, North Korea.

"Good morning, Tom. Thank you for reaching out. Let me be brief," Director Parks said.

"No problem. What is on your mind?" Tom responded.

"I'm flying to Havana, Cuba, on Monday with a stopover in Mexico City. Please meet me in front of the Mexico City airport's MacDonald's restaurant at two p.m. There is only one. Please bring Ruth with you."

"Mexico City airport's MacDonald's on Monday at two p.m. with Ruth. Is there anything else that you want to share?"

"No. It's best that we speak face to face."

"Very good. See you on Monday."

§

Thursday Tom received clearance to travel to Mexico City along with a small security escort. He called his contact in the Mexican *Policía Federal Ministerial,* commonly referred to as the PFM, and asked for cooperation in planning security for the meeting on Monday. After making a few inquiries, he then arranged for a driver to take him downtown to catch Ruth as she walked home from class.

Arriving downtown, Tom immediately spotted Ruth and lowered his car window as she walked along the street. "May I offer you a ride?"

Without uttering a word, Ruth walked over to the car and got in. "I take it that you spoke with Director Parks."

"Yes. He asked that the two of us fly to Mexico City and meet him on Monday at the airport while he waits for a stopover flight. May I offer you a free trip to

Mexico City leaving Sunday afternoon returning Tuesday evening?"

"Sounds like fun."

"This is for expenses." Tom handed her a credit card. "I'll email you ticket information. In view of the urgency and security concerns, we have been cleared to fly business class, ostensively as consultants for the Federal Reserve. If anyone asks, we're traveling to Mexico to brief the Central Bank on recent bank failures. I'm an assistant to a board member, and you are my speechwriter." Tom handed her a red, administrative U.S. passport.

"Wow. You are efficient. What if I had said no?" Ruth chuckled. "Do I need to bring anything special?"

"Just carryon baggage with the needed clothes for a three-day trip. I'll pick you up with a car at noon on Sunday and brief you on what you need to know."

The car pulled up in front of Ruth's dorm, and she got out. "See you Sunday."

"Bye for now. Sorry to mess up your schedule and studies."

Chapter 12

Thursday evening Luke called Ruth.

"Hello Luke?"

"How are you? Did you enjoy *Mardi Gras*? When are you going to share photos from the party?"

"I trust my photographer to pick the best photos for magazine publication and don't otherwise pay much attention."

"What? So, I'll need to buy a Korean language magazine to see your pictures?"

"Okay. I'll ask him to send me proofs and share them when they arrive."

"Sounds good. Say, do you want to get together this weekend?"

"What? Are you inviting me to run laps with you and spot you in the weight-room with all those smelly guys?"

"Ha. Ha. I was hoping for something a bit more fun."

"How about we catch a quick lunch on Saturday

in Georgetown? My schedule is a bit tight this week.

"Okay. How about checking out that pizza joint that you keep telling me about?"

"Great. Pick me up at eleven?"

"Super. See you then."

§

Saturday morning, Luke picked up Ruth and drove her to the pizza place. He placed their order and found a table near the window to sit down to talk.

"How is your training coming along? Have you met the standards required in the physical screening test?" Ruth asked.

"Actually, I did, but just barely. I'm training so hard that I'm having trouble keeping my weight up. I'm really lusting after this pizza."

"What about the firearm training? Are you comfortable firing the standard issue Glock, Remington 12-gauge, and AR-15?"

"I'm surprised that you are familiar with these requirements. Most women, even in the military, are not especially excited about firearms. But to answer your question, more recent models have a wider range of features and handle a bit differently, but a gun is a gun. Even with the same weapons, however, the training is as different as are the legal environments."

Ruth spoke with Luke over pizza for about an hour, but she avoided the issue of Mexico City and complications that Luke wasn't yet ready for. *Why should I upset Luke during the little time that we have together?*

Chapter 13

Sunday afternoon, Tom picked up Ruth exactly at noon, and the driver took them to Washington Dulles International Airport, about a thirty-minute drive. Tom outlined the details of the meeting with Director Parks.

"Director Parks will be accompanied by a security detail that he likely hopes to distract from our conversation. This is probably why he asked for you to come along."

"Me? Why me?"

"For whatever reason, he trusts you."

"Okay. If you say so."

"Anyhow, here is our strategy. Our security team will stake out the McDonalds before Director Parks arrives and signal when he is in position. I'll then go to get in position near him; you will follow thirty seconds behind me. While you distract his security team, he and I'll talk. When we're done, my security team will extract you and we will meet up at the rendezvous point, likely near the airport security office. Ideally, at no point will people observe you and me together or Director Parks and me, which will secure our conversation and persons."

"Sounds like a plan. Will the security teams be armed?"

"No. The restaurant is inside airport security so only the Mexican police will be armed."

"That's a relief. Creating a scene is one thing; worrying about trigger-happy guards is another."

"For sure."

§

The flight to Mexico City was on time. Having red passports eased the trip through security. Tom chuckled to himself as Ruth watched out the window at the tenements, slums and shanties that stretched for miles during the approach to *Aeropuerto Internacional Benito Juárez,* known in English as Mexico City International Airport. They arrived in Mexico City and deplaned around ten a.m., which allowed plenty of time to enjoy a leisurely lunch with the security team, walk the concourse, and rehearse their strategy.

At quarter to two, Tom was alerted by his security detail.

"Director Parks is seated at a table across from the McDonald's with a middle-aged woman and is escorted by a single security officer. They are both dressed like tourists. The Director is wearing a Hawaiian shirt, blue sunglasses, and white pants with a camera around his neck. The woman is also wearing a Hawaiian shirt with a matching white skirt, but looks too nervous to be a tourist," the security officer reported through his headset.

"Okay. I'm moving into position," Tom said, also through a headset.

"I'm right behind you and will walk in once you get into line for an order," Ruth said, likewise through the headset.

Tom walked down the concourse and got into line at the McDonalds. Ruth then proceeded down the concourse. When she got close to the McDonald's, she recognized the woman with Director Parks.

"MOM. MOM, it's me," Ruth shouted in Korean.

The woman jumped up and began running down the concourse towards Ruth. "YONG DAE. YONG DAE," she shouted using Ruth's Korean name.

Director Parks pointed to his security officer and told him: "Watch them. Don't let them run off." The officer ran down the concourse towards the women, who continued to shout and cry.

Meanwhile, Director Parks walked over to Tom and pretended to be in line at the McDonald's.

"Tom, thanks for coming. Time is short. China intends to invade Taiwan in late August or early September. I'm traveling to Havana to enlist their support in a diversionary attack on major Caribbean and Atlantic ports. Look for ships delivering pop-up mine components traveling to Cuban ports."

"Pop-up mines?"

"Yes. The sinking of the New Moon was proof of concept. The idea is to seed the waters outside major ports with these mines that will be triggered to arm just before major hurricanes. Ships staying in port will be pounded by the hurricanes. Those leaving will encounter the mines. The chaos that ensues will delay reinforcing Taiwan with military supplies. Got to go."

Director Parks walked back over to the table where he had been sitting and sat down. He signaled his security officer to return. "Leave the woman. Let's go." The two then left.

Tom ordered an ice cream cone and returned to his seat to wait for Ruth and her mother to settle down.

Chapter 14

Tuesday, Tom flew back to the United States with Ruth and her mother. He arranged for a CIA team to pick them up at Washington Dulles International Airport and take them to a hotel to relax so that he could debrief them on their experience in Mexico City. Director Parks had asked Ruth's mom to help him pose as a Korean couple visiting Havana on vacation, so there was not much to tell.

"Why did Director Parks bring my mother—an old housewife—on this trip?" Ruth asked Tom.

"We can only speculate, but my guess is that he knew you were close to your mother and wanted to strengthen his relationship with you without the usual coercion, which is most curious."

"Why? I have nothing to offer him. It's normally a serious offense assisting a North Korean citizen to defect."

"Why indeed?" Tom repeated.

After spending the night in the hotel, Ruth's uncle, Pastor Chŭ, stopped by and drove her mom to his home. Ruth returned to the dorm at school.

§

Wednesday morning, Tom met with the debriefing team and CIA Director Jeremiah Peters to go over the meeting with RGB Director Parks.

"What do you make of Parks' revelation of his mission in Havana? Is China really prepared to invade Taiwan?" The director asked.

"Director Parks claims that the New Moon sinking is proof of Beijing's seriousness."

"Has this claim been corroborated?"

"No, but Parks has done two unprecedented things. He provided us sensitive intelligence about Beijing's intentions and he assisted Mrs. Chŭ in defecting. The two things are related. Mrs. Chŭ's release is like an exclamation point on the intelligence. I take it as his way of saying that this intelligence is genuine because he has no other motive for releasing Mrs. Chŭ into our custody," Tom responded.

"I agree. He must be flagging North Korea's

concern about a possible Taiwanese invasion. War in the pacific would be unsettling for many in the region even if they cannot or will not openly oppose China's action," the director opined.

"Director Parks must anticipate that the CIA will want to confirm what he has said, which will no doubt be picked up by Chinese state security when they get closer to the truth. Perhaps, he is hoping that China will back off if their plans became known," Tom said.

"I think that you have hit on something there. I'm starting to like this guy."

"Me too. He is as bright as they come."

"Obviously, we have our work cut out for us here. Let's see what we can do to get China to put this plan on the back burner." The director stood and left the room.

As the debriefing team got up to leave, Tom asked. "What is a pop-up mine?"

"No idea," one team member responded. "You need to visit with the naval research team."

"Crazy Roscoes' group at the model basin?"

"Oh, you've been there before?"

§

Tom called down to the motor pool and requested a car to drive him to the model basin in Potomac, Maryland. Then he walked out to the office secretary.

"Can you get Roscoe Billings on a secure phone?"

"Give me a minute," the secretary responded. "Pick up on line one."

"Hello, Roscoe? This is Tom Roberts at Langley. I have priority topic to go over with you in person. Be there in about thirty minutes."

"No chance of that—allow forty-five minutes. I'll be ready when you arrive. What's the subject?" Roscoe responded.

"I'll go over that when I arrive," Tom said.

"You are always so cloak and dagger."

"That's me."

§

Tom arrived at the model basin a bit late, just as Roscoe predicted. He badged his way through the security gate and into the building, walking past a number of smartly-crafted submarine and surface ship models displayed in front of Roscoe's office.

"Knock, knock," Tom said, entering the office.

"What have you got?" Roscoe asked.

Tom closed the office door and pulled up a chair next to Roscoe's desk, close enough to whisper. "What is a pop-up mine?"

"Pop-up mine? Are you kidding me?"

"Did I say something wrong?" Tom responded.

"I have never actually seen one. A pop-up mine is a sort of internet-concept weapon. I call them the IED of naval junk bombs."

"Junk bombs?" Tom echoed.

"Yeah. You take a couple of bath tubs, fill them with whatever explosives are handy, strap them together back-to-back, weigh them down so they sink, and toss them in the ocean wrapped with a receiver/balloon contraption. When the receiver is activated, the balloon inflates and the bomb rises to the prescribed depth to wait for a programmed audio-signature of a particular prop and intensity. The targeted ship steams by and boom."

"A custom, low-tech, water bomb?" Tom paraphrased.

"Basically. The hard part comes in collecting the audio signatures and testing proof of concept. No one has actually implemented one of these things that we know about. What makes this thing a threat is that it basically looks like floating junk and would remain undetectable on the ocean floor until activated."

"What if they skip the audio signatures and just trigger on intensity?"

"Then you would have a terrorist weapon."

"Bingo. A basement bomb buildable by any determined group of terrorists."

"Pretty much. Where did you hear about these things."

"What does the Navy say happened to the New Moon?" Tom asked.

"The investigation is ongoing—are you saying that the New Moon was sunk by a pop-up mine?

"I cannot say. You know the drill. If anyone asks,

just say I know a kid with an internet connection and a fridge full of beer."

"You're no fun."

"Total party-pooper. Anyhow, thanks for your help. If you hear anything further about pop-up mines—even if it's only internet chatter—anything at all, call me immediately. This is a priority issue."

"While you are here, let me pass on a couple of items that worry us here that may be pertinent to your pop-up mines."

"Go on."

"First, an internet site that purports to be interested in saving the whales has been posting acoustical files on naval ships, especially U.S. ships. When we try to track down where this site originates, it moves. Our best guess is Lebanon, thanks to a tip from the Israel's Mossad."

"That's disturbing."

Second, a small toy company, called Tianchi Toy, located next to Heaven Lake on the boarder of Manchuria and North Korea recently ordered a large batch of titanium, which is the best metal for making seawater-resistant parts. Heaven Lake is deep enough to test the receiver parts for a pop-up mine and remote enough not to be easily observed. It also lies adjacent to Paektu Mountain where Kim Jong-Il, the founder of North Korea, claimed to have been born."

"Yikes. Is that everything?"

"Just one thing more. A titanium receiver could be little bigger than twice the size of a cell-phone because the sensors and receiver could be programmed into a chip. The hard part for engineers would be crafting a watertight, deep-water compartment for the chip, battery, and leads to the balloon and detonation fuse. The balloon could be inflated with something as small as a CO_2 canister for an air gun. The only real tell for pop-up mine observable from a distance would be an inordinate interest in bath tubs. The weakness of this concept would be the battery life of the receiver. Most batteries for such components are only good for a year or two."

"Thanks. This is most helpful intel."

"You are welcome. Let me know if you learn anything or if you have any further questions."

"Sure. Why do people call you Crazy Roscoe?"

"It started as a comment on my musical taste at the academy—as an African-American kid, I used to dabble in rap. Later, Crazy became my handle in the Seals."

Chapter 15

On the way to Wednesday classes, Ruth noticed that someone was following her. On reaching the corner of her class building, she ran to conceal herself behind a car across the street to observe who this might be. When she peered into the mirror of the car, she saw an anguished Lei Han run around the corner and look around frantically. When he realized he had lost her, he slowed down and walked off.

Ruth took photographs of him with her cell-phone and followed him down the street until he got in a car and drove off. She took photos of his car to record his license number and returned to class, which had not yet started.

Ruth texted Tom, along with the photos.

Ruth: *At Luke's reception last week I thought that I saw Lei Han. Now today, I caught him following me around campus. Am I hallucinating?*

Several minutes passed.

Tom: *No. You are not hallucinating. Your photos*

confirm Lei Han's identity. The car that you spotted was reported stolen two days ago, which is consistent with someone trying to avoid detection.

Ruth: *Oh, good. Thanks. Got to go. My class is starting.*

§

When Ruth's class finished, she turned to leave as Lei Han approached her. She sat back down.

"We need to talk." Lei Han sat next to her, speaking Korean quietly to avoid listening ears.

"About what? I thought you were in a Chinese prison." Ruth responded.

"Things change, and here I am."

"What do you want?"

"Director Parks wants you to help me find a security leak."

"That's a lie. You work for Chinese state security, not the RGB. Director Parks would never send you to contact me."

"You are too smart for your own good," Lei Han blurted out. "Your boyfriend, Luke, is just dating you to make Abi Ling jealous."

"What do you know about Luke or Abi? Did she finally realize her mistake in leaving Luke for you? You are the jealous one."

Lei Han jumped up and stomped off, leaving Ruth sitting in her desk frowning and mumbling to herself as students began to file in for the next class. *Is it true. Does Luke really want to get back with Abi? How does Lei Han know that Luke and I are dating?*

§

Thursday evening, Ruth called Luke. "My mother defected this week and now lives with my uncle here in Northern Virginia."

"Really? How did that happen?"

"It's a long story and I have yet to learn all the details. In any case, she would like to meet you. Are you available to come over on Sunday after church for lunch with us?"

"Absolutely. Should I swing by and pick you up at school?"

"No. I'm going over early to hear my uncle

preach. You can join us once you finish up with services at your church."

"What time?"

"Come when you are ready. My uncle's congregation pretty much spends the entire day with one another, including a late lunch. I hope that you like Korean food."

"If it's with you, I'll love it. Should I bring anything?"

"Yes. It's customary for guests to bring a small, wrapped gift when they first meet, especially when it involves parents."

"Would your mother like a silk scarf?"

"That's a great idea. Red and yellow are her favorite colors."

"I'll see what I can do. See you Sunday."

"Luke. Let me change the subject briefly."

"Sure. What's up?"

"Do you have a telephone number for Abi? I would like to check in on her."

"I have her old number, but I have no idea

whether she still uses it. I'll text it to you."

§

Ruth received Luke's text with Abi Ling's telephone number and dialed it, wondering if the daughter of the Chinese Premier would answer her own phone, even if she were a medical student in Baltimore.

"Hello, Abi, this is Ruth. How are you?"

"Ruth, I'm surprised that you have the nerve to call me. What's this about?"

"I apologize for calling you on a week night. Lei Han approached me in class this afternoon, which seemed odd. I was wondering why he is here in DC. I thought that he was in a Chinese prison."

"He was. His friends sprung him loose."

"Are you still in touch with him?"

"No. I made a big mistake in getting back with him and broke off our relationship months ago. I haven't seen or heard from him since I left Beijing."

"Are you still seeing Luke?"

"No. He has not called me. Why do you ask?"

"Lei Han inferred that you were still interested

in Luke."

"He would. He is one of the most jealous men that I have ever known. I broke up with Luke in Beijing before hanging out with Lei Han, and that was the last time that we communicated."

"Okay, thanks."

"Are you seeing Luke?"

"We have gone out a few times."

"I see. Give him my best."

Chapter 16

Luke preached at both services on Jesus' baptism and sojourn in the desert in the Gospel of Mark. The sermon title was *Relying on God*. While the sermon focused on the deprivations and temptations of the people of Israel in the desert, his own escape from North Korea with Ruth a few weeks prior loomed large in his thinking.

After shaking a few hands, Luke finished up his pastoral duties and drove to Pastor Chŭ's church in Leesburg, Virginia. He arrived at one p.m., but the parking lot was full. He spent fifteen minutes driving down the street and looking for a parking space.

When he finally arrived, he hurried through the door holding a present wrapped in candy cane colored foil tied up with a white ribbon bow, embarrassed that his gift might seem like an ostentatious peace offering for a late arrival. He found Ruth and her mom waiting undisturbed on a hallway bench and in no hurry as if a sacrifice of time were no sacrifice at all. *Wow. Korean time is measured in decades, not Washingtonian milliseconds or even New York minutes.*

Luke noticed—how could he not notice?—that Ruth's mother wore a red silk dress, looking like a woman in her twenties that had never tasted a dumpling. Her hair had been dyed jet black and permed. She sported bright red lipstick and one might have taken her to be Ruth's older sister, but for the crow's feet around her sparkling green eyes.

"How did your sermon go?" Ruth asked as she stood.

"No one fell asleep, but I did see a couple of heads start to bob," Luke said before holding up his gift. "This is for your mom." Luke handed her the present.

"Tank you," Ruth's mom smiled and bowed.

"Did you have a good trip from Korea?" Luke asked.

Ruth translated Luke's question to her mother, who grinned, bowing her head and responding in Korean to Ruth.

"Mom says her trip was long and scary. She did not know that she was coming to America until it happened," Ruth translated.

"Perhaps after lunch you can tell me your mother's story," Luke said, trying to avoid keeping them any longer from eating.

"Sure thing. Let's go join the others."

§

Luke walked with Ruth, who held her mother's hand as they proceeded down the hall into fellowship hall. There, Luke recognized Pastor Chŭ and his family sitting at the head table.

Pastor Chŭ stood to welcome Luke, Ruth, and her mother to sit with them. "Good to see you again. I hope that you are settled back into your normal routine after all the excitement from your ordeal this past fall."

"It has been hard to get over my unplanned tour of North Korea, but it does feel good to be home again. How are you and your sister getting along? It must be a shock to be reunited with family after so many years of separation," Luke said.

"Yes. You are most observant. Our dilemma is fairly common in the Korean community, so we get plenty of help from others who know what we have been through."

After lunch Luke drove Ruth back to school.

§

During the trip from Leesburg, Virginia to downtown Washington, Luke drove in silence.

"What's up, Ruth? You seem distracted this evening," Luke asked.

"My mother told me that after you and I left Najin in October, my father was murdered at sea, most likely by a North Korean patrol boat. His boat full of bullet holes and missing the engine washed ashore on a Japanese beach. I'm having trouble processing everything."

"Oh, no. Your father must have died during the voyage down close to South Korea. He used my cellphone to send a text to Abi and divert attention away from us while we escaped over the border into China.

He planned this diversion and must have died executing it. I owe him my life. You owe him your freedom."

Ruth froze, stunned by Luke's words. After a few moments, her head dropped down and she began to sob quietly. "Oh, Father. Oh, Father."

Luke drove silently across the Key Bridge into Georgetown. When he reached Ruth's dorm, he parked the car and just sat without saying a word. After a few minutes, Ruth excused herself and left.

Chapter 17

Sunday evening, Ruth called her mother.

"Why didn't Dad tell me that he was sailing near South Korea waters?"

"He knew he might not come back and he wanted to help you escape into China. His trip south misled those seeking Mr. Stevens long enough for you to cross the border safely. He asked Mr. Stevens to assist you in coming to America—it was part of the deal he had your grandfather negotiate."

"Deal? I don't understand. You and Dad arranged for me to marry the Supreme Leader's nephew in exchange for the fishing boat, which seemed uncaring and callous to me at the time. I understand now that this arrangement was less than voluntary, but why the sudden concern about my welfare?"

"Your father never forgave himself for arranging your marriage and was extremely proud of your success as a law student. His old navy buddies remained dangerously jealous both about your success and the boat. They harassed him at sea for years and probably killed him out of pure spite."

"Some things never change, no matter what the Supreme Leader says or does. Trading a Mao jacket for a banker's suit coat and now an aviator's leather jacket and sunglasses does not change daily life in the Hermit Kingdom... Oh, Mom. Oh, Mom." Ruth pined.

"Ruth, tell me about you and Mr. Stevens. Has he proposed to you?"

"I thought you wanted me to find a nice Korean boy."

"In your engagement to the Supreme Leader's nephew, you proved yourself a loyal and faithful daughter. Now who you marry is your concern."

'Thank you, Mom."

ACT THREE

Chapter 18

Over the next week, Luke prepared for training at Quantico. He tried contacting Ruth several times, but she never picked up or responded to his texts. On the first Monday in March, he reported to the base to begin school.

For Luke, the check-in procedure at the FBI Academy felt like a cross between a first day at college and reporting for Army bootcamp. Students were, of course, older and more mature, most being college graduates, and a fair portion had military service. Smiling faces and contagious enthusiasm permeated the atmosphere as students hurried from station to station picking up uniforms, piecing together gear, and having photos taken for IDs. If any nervousness arose, it focused on passing the physical fitness test (PFT)—the sit-ups, the 300-meter sprint, push-ups, the 1.5 mile-timed run, and the pull-ups—but judging by the buff crowd present, such fears were misplaced.

Standing in line, Luke noticed a familiar silhouette and head of hair in front of him. "Natalie. What are you doing here?"

"You do know a future special FBI agent when you see one, don't you?" Natalie responded.

"Are you kidding? I thought you were still in high school—McLean or Langley—right?"

"I'm shocked and appalled. Don't you know a college graduate when you see one?"

"Am I so old that I cannot judge students' ages anymore?" Luke said.

"I'm messing with you—I'm still nineteen. I had to get special approval to sign up for FBI training because of my age. What about you? What are you doing here? Aren't you a pastor anymore?"

"Actually, I'm a bi-vocational pastor. I used to tell people I was a tentmaker like the Apostle Paul, but many people are not biblically literate, so now I just say that I'm a volunteer or part-time pastor to save time."

"If you are bi-vocational, what do you do during the week?"

"You grew up in McLean, right? I work for the highway commission."

"Highway commission? You are such a tease—that sign came down years ago."

"So you do know what Langley is famous for!"

"Hard to image that you have never seen a television spy drama. I'm just shocked to hear that my pastor has a second job."

"Okay, future special FBI agent. Mum's the word."

§

Luke made his rounds of the stations getting checked in. Having been assigned a dorm room, he stowed his things, put on his uniform—khaki pants and a black FBI Academy polo—and caught some lunch in the cafeteria before attending the orientation ceremony. After a two-hour overview of expectations and a brief summary of the training calendar, he was instructed to report to the gym to begin taking his physical fitness test (PFT). When he ran into Natalie on the way to the gym, he wished he had skipped lunch.

"Are you ready for the PFT?" Natalie asked.

"Pretty much. My trainer estimated that I would

probably score about twenty points on the test, but I'm wondering now if lunch was a great idea—twelve points may be a challenge. How about you?"

"You had a trainer?"

"Yes. My office was not optimistic that I would pass the PFT and assigned me a trainer and time to work out."

"Wow. Must be nice. I haven't worried much about the test. I play a lot of soccer and am used to running intervals. Thirty points may be about right."

"Oooooo. I'm impressed. I've seen you run, but I did not know that you played soccer. What position do you play?"

"Normally, I've no competition in playing half-back. Most of the rest of the team has trouble sprinting the length of the field over and over."

"Good for you. I played stopper in graduate school," Luke said as he held the gym door open for Natalie.

Natalie walked through the door and turned. "Luke, did you drive down from McLean?"

"Yes. Why?"

"Can I catch a ride back with you on Friday? Otherwise, my mom will need to drive down to pick me up—it's kind of a pain for her."

"Sure. No problem." Luke wrote down his cell number and handed it to her. "Text me when you are ready to leave. Otherwise, see you on the far side."

Monday afternoon, Luke passed his PFT achieving a score of twenty-five, exceeding expectations. That night, dinner never tasted so good and he slept soundly through the night.

§

Tuesday morning, Luke's first class met at eight.

The presenter began with atomic precision at eight. "While the promotional videos for the FBI Academy focus on the hands-on and stressful aspects of an agent's training, trainees have to learn about the objectives, standard-operating procedures, and legal aspects of law enforcement up front. The protocols for every operation may sound boring, but knowing them inside and out will save you a lot of sleepless nights and may save your life."

Luke took voluminous notes. Looking around the room, he saw that he was not alone. The lectures had the full attention of trainees all morning. By eleven o'clock, however, people began looking around and checking their watches with lunch calling their names.

Chapter 19

Ruth left her morning class to find her green tan suit colleagues waiting outside. They nervously walked up to her.

The man blurted out. "We need to talk."

Ruth sensed a panic in his voice. "What's up?"

"A man calling himself Lei Han has replaced Director Parks, who disappeared during a visit to Havana. Director Han asked you to report in."

"Report in? How am I supposed to do that?"

The man handed her a cell phone, "This phone is secure. Call as soon as possible."

"I understand," Ruth responded, taking the phone.

The man and woman bowed, turned, and left.

Ruth put the phone in her purse and walked to her dorm, forgetting her usual luncheon stop at the cafeteria.

Reaching her dorm room, Ruth shut the door and called Tom.

"Hello, Tom? This is Ruth. Do you have a minute?"

"Absolutely. What's up?"

"We have a problem. I just learned that Director Parks has disappeared in Havana, and Lei Han has replaced him as RGB Director. This could not be good."

"No kidding? How did you learn about this?"

"Lei Han sent a team to meet me and gave me a secure cell to call in."

"Really?"

"There is more. Last Wednesday after I texted you Lei Han's photograph, he approached me after class and tried to recruit me to find a security leak. I sent him away, but he must have already taken over the Director's position then. How else how would he have known how to find me or cared about a leak?"

"You may be right. Is there anything else I should know?"

"No. I'm just concerned about Director Parks. He is a good man."

"One hopes that he has been able to find sanctuary somewhere."

"That would be best. Should I call Lei Han? Is he really RGB Director?"

"I'll try to find out and let you know—hold off calling him until I can find out."

"I will. Let me know as soon as possible."

"I'll call later this afternoon, if I can."

"Thanks."

Ruth put her phone back in her purse and left to get some lunch.

Chapter 20

Tuesday afternoon, Tom made inquiries among analysts in his office, but none knew anything about Director Parks' status or about Lei Han's ascendancy to the director's position. Concerned that this development ominously dovetailed with his conversation with Director Parks in Mexico City, he made an appointment to visit the CIA director, Jeremiah Peters, who asked him to report to his office immediately.

When Tom walked into his office, the director was waiting for him.

"Tom, what do you have for me?"

"Sir, I want permission to validate some intel about a leadership transition in North Korea."

"What have you heard?"

"The rumor is that RGB Director Parks has disappeared and been replaced by a Chinese operative, Lei Han."

"Lei Han? I thought he was in a Chinese prison for downing that airliner over the Sea of Japan last fall."

"Apparently, his prison stay was short. Before this rumor came up, he was sighted by several people here in McLean and also in DC. For a while we had him under observation, but he evaded us and he keeps turning up like a bad penny."

"What is your source for his RGB appointment?"

"Lei Han has been working to turn Ruth Chǔ into an asset, most recently by claiming that he replaced her old boss."

"This is serious. What do you propose?"

"I would like permission to call my friend, Harry Bai."

"The Chinese Minister of State Security?"

"Yes. Because of recent tensions, Harry cannot talk about much, but he will probably be willing to confirm or deny Lei Han's assertion."

"What will you give in return?"

"Harry is personally interested in Abi Ling's security. She remains a student in Baltimore, so we can offer assistance."

"The Premier's daughter?"

"Yes. Harry is close to the Premier and has long worked to keep Abi safe."

"Okay. Reach out to Harry, but keep the conversation brief and on point."

Tom shook the director's hand and left.

§

At five p.m., Tom pulled a secure cell phone out of his desk that Harry had given him earlier.

"Harry, this is Tom. I apologize for calling you so early in the morning."

"I know you wouldn't call unless it were important."

"Thank you. What is the latest on Lei Han?"

"Lei Han? Why do you ask?"

"He showed up here in DC last week."

"Most curious. He is a trouble maker and tied to recent changes here in Beijing."

"Has he replaced RGB Director Parks in North Korea?"

"There is an unconfirmed rumor to that effect.

How did you hear about it?"

"He made that claim this week in pressuring our mutual friend, Ruth Chǔ."

"Thanks for telling me. Lei Han may be trying to use Ruth to track Luke or, perhaps, to pressure the Premier through Abi." Harry paused. "I really should not be talking to you, as you are probably aware."

"I appreciate your willingness to take my call. I'll continue to keep an eye on Abi Ling."

"You are the best—we really do make a good team." Harry hung up the phone.

§

As soon as Harry hung up, Tom dialed Ruth's number.

"Ruth, this is Tom."

"What did you learn?"

"There is a good chance Lei Han is telling the truth about replacing Director Parks. The full truth may be a bit more slippery. The political situation in Beijing currently moves too fast for most players to keep up."

"I understand. Thanks, Tom."

§

Wednesday morning, Tom called the director of the FBI Academy, Roger Smith.

"Roger, how are you?"

"I'm good. It's been a while. What keeps you busy?"

"Highway Commission stuff. You know the drill."

"Sure. What can I do for you?"

"I've a question about my analyst, Luke Steven's, schedule. When does he start firearms training?"

"Oh, that's easy. The basic orientation begins this afternoon on the shooting range. We like to start off trainees early and keep them practicing throughout the program. Why do you ask?"

"We're likely to have an all-hands drill in the near future and I'll need Luke in the field. I cannot in good conscience send him out without basic knowledge how to keep his head in a fight, managing firearms, and shoot."

"I understand. We work hard to teach trainees situational awareness—Luke was the guy that escaped North Korea last fall, right?"

"You remember. He has more field experience than many of my agents, just not in the role of an agent."

"Interesting way to put it—I suspect that situational awareness will be natural for him."

"Yeah—a little fear goes a long way. Anyhow, thanks for the details. I'll get back to you if I need to pull Luke out early."

Chapter 21

Late Tuesday, Luke attended a scheduled lecture featuring Roscoe Billings on working as an analyst in an intelligence agency.

Roscoe began with a statement of principle. "Success in intelligence analysis arises with understanding the word: misfit. Look for items and observations that don't fit with their surroundings. Misfits. Some are obvious; many aren't."

A hand went up and Roscoe pointed at her. "Can you give us an example?"

"Certainly. This past week, we noticed a toy company placing a large order for titanium. Can anyone tell me why that might be interesting?"

Another hand went up. Roscoe nodded.

"Titanium is too expensive to use in toy production," a student said.

"Bingo. What else?"

Luke looked around to see a lot of blank looks on student faces.

Roscoe continued: "My specialty is naval research. Titanium is one of the best materials for making things that won't rust in seawater. Other good metals to use on boats are brass, bronze, 316 stainless steel, and aluminum. My ears stand up when anyone mentions titanium because it's the Cadillac of ocean-ready metals."

"Ohooooooo," the students exhaled.

"When we looked into this toy company order, we found this company located in a remote area next to a deep-water lake. In my line of work, that location suggested an interest in clandestine naval research. Anyhow, the titanium find provided an excellent application of the misfit principle."

§

Friday evening, Luke turned his cell phone on and texted Natalie.

Luke: *Are you ready to leave?*

Natalie: *Slow poke. I'm waiting by your car.*

Luke: *Give me five.*

Luke scrolled through his messages and found a text from Ruth.

Ruth: *Sorry that I've been out of touch. I'm* still *dealing with my dad's passing. Give me a call when you are free.*

Luke: *I'm getting ready to leave Quantico. Call me if you are free.*

Luke grabbed his laundry bag and backpack with his laptop and walked towards his car where Natalie was waving at him.

"How was your week?" Luke asked.

"My week was good. I scored thirty on the PFT, as expected. How about you?"

"I exceeded expectation at twenty-five points. Are you ready for a little 95 traffic?"

"Sure. I even brought my pillow."

§

Luke got into the car, put on his seat belt, and checked to see if Natalie was buckled in. All secure, he started the car, backed out, and started driving. No sooner than he left campus, when his cell phone buzzed and the hands-free feature of his car kicked in.

"Luke, this is Ruth. How was your week?"

"Invigorating. I'll sleep well this weekend. How was your week?"

"I've been nervous and upset all week between my dad's passing and the news about Director Parks, who has disappeared. Now, Lei Han claims to be his replacement. Does that make any sense at all?"

"Ruth, I'm driving back to McLean with a friend from school. Do you remember Natalie from my church? She is training to be an FBI special agent and shares some of my classes."

"Really?"

"Ruth? How are you? How's school?" Natalie responded.

"Natalie, what is this I hear about you taking classes with Luke? Aren't you like nineteen?"

"Yes, I am, but I just graduated from college and got an age-exemption to join the FBI."

"Wow. That's impressive. Congratulations. So now you are going to follow your mother's advice and date Luke?"

"No current plans—I'm just going to school—

nothing more. You worry too much."

Ruth hung up.

Luke redialed Ruth's number, but no one answered.

"I'm so sorry."

"It's not your fault. Ruth has a lot on her mind this week. I'll call her back later."

§

Stuck in traffic on Interstate 95, Natalie said nothing for half an hour.

"I feel really bad about making trouble for you with Ruth," Natalie confessed.

"It's not your fault. Ruth recently lost her dad and now she has to deal with a nasty development back home in North Korea."

"May I ask you a personal question?"

"What's that?"

"Should I call you Luke or do you prefer Phil?"

Luke looked at Natalie like he had seen a ghost. "What kind of question is that?"

You don't need to answer if you don't want to."

Luke thought for a moment. "Luke has been my legal name since my son was killed in Baltimore by North Korean terrorists. My office had me go undercover to flush out the terrorists, some of whom are still at large. How did you know?"

"I've known both of you well for years. You and your son looked so much alike that the only real differences arose in personalities: You are a serious guy; Luke was more fun."

"Thank you for that. Please don't tell anyone. If anyone asks, I'm Luke, the former Navy Seal and CIA analyst. Only a handful of close colleagues know my identity."

"No problem. I have a security clearance and will soon be an FBI special agent."

"Right. Thanks. Just so you know, Ruth still does not know my whole story. It has been hard to share it with her because she still has a foot in two worlds and could easily be blackmailed."

"I understand. At some point, you will need to let her know."

"Yes. I know. I'm not used to the world of secrets that I find myself in. Pastors normally live totally exposed in the city square. It's one of the burdens that we bear."

"So you actually passed the PFT at age fifty-two?"

"Actually, I did. The FBI Academy has no idea that I'm undercover."

"Wow. You are one badass pastor."

Chapter 22

Friday evening, Luke called Ruth, who picked up after five rings.

"Hey. Sorry about this afternoon. I over-reacted," Ruth started.

"Are you okay? I'm worried about you," Luke said.

"I've had better days, better weeks."

"Do you want to do something together this weekend?"

"No. I can't. Classes are pretty intense right now, but the pastor who was supposed to preach Sunday morning for the Korean Alliance can't make it, and we can't find a replacement. Would you like to preach for us? You get a free lunch out of the deal."

"Actually, I'm on leave of absence from church until I finish my training, so I'm available. What is the sermon text?"

"We have been studying the prophets. This week is supposed to focus on the Prophet Jonah."

"Super. I love Jonah. He was so real about hating Ninevites. What time should I pick you up?"

"Be here at ten, and we can walk over together."

"Sounds like a date. What's the dress code for pastors?"

"Anything you like. Just don't embarrass me and show up all California with a butch haircut and earring, dressed in black."

"What's that about?"

"Inside joke. See you Sunday."

§

Sunday morning, Luke dressed in a blue blazer with red tie and white shirt before driving downtown to DC. There he parked on Ruth's street, texted his arrival, and walked up to her dorm where she met him at the front door.

"So punctual, exactly at ten a.m.," Ruth teased him as they walked to the student union cafeteria.

"How are you this morning?"

"I'm feeling better. Yesterday, I actually focused on my studies."

"Good. Myself, I was exhausted and slept in. Wake me if you catch me sleeping on my feet."

"Hey, the congregation is supposed to sleep, not the pastor."

"Details, details," Luke said as he pushed the door open to the student union.

As they entered the cafeteria, they found close to forty students waiting for them, anxious to meet the famous pastor whom Ruth had smuggled out of North Korea. Luke found himself struggling to shake hands on the way in. Usually pastors shake hands at the end of the service as a way to slow people down as they head for the door.

Ruth took Luke by the hand and walked him over to the impromptu pulpit that had been set up, had him sit down behind it, and handed him a printed bulletin. She then asked everyone to have a seat. A small stage band began playing *What a Friend We Have in Jesus*. Luke was surprised to hear a familiar hymn rather than the more contemporary music that most churches focus on. When the music stopped, Ruth welcomed everyone and shared some announcements. One of the students then came up and read from the first three verses of the first chapter of the Book of Jonah:

> Now the word of the LORD came to Jonah the son of Amittai, saying, Arise, go to Nineveh, that great city, and call out against it, for their evil has come up before me. But Jonah rose to flee to Tarshish from the presence of the LORD.

After finishing the reading, the student turned to Luke to cue him to begin the sermon.

"I want to thank everyone who made it possible for me to be with you this morning." Luke began. He then gave a short description of his recent trip to North Korea. "Our text today from the Prophet Jonah is timely and pointed. The question posed by scripture when we witness sin and societal decay is: Are we in the community of faith going to pray for sinners like Abraham witnessing Sodom and Gomorrah or run away from our prophetic duty like the Prophet Jonah?"

Luke could see from their faces that he had their attention.

Luke went on to cite the five attributes of God

himself—mercy, grace, patience, love, and faithfulness—that God gave Moses after the second giving of the law on Mount Sinai. He then argued that God's first attribute is mercy. Jonah feared that the Ninevites would repent of their sin and God would forgive them. God's mercy is the lens through which we experience God's love through Jesus Christ.

After the sermon and a quick lunch, Ruth asked Luke to take her home. On the way, she stopped: "Why didn't you tell me about your son dying in Baltimore? We both lost someone there."

Luke looked up, then down. "I have been undercover since Baltimore, and it is not my story to tell."

"So, Abi knows?"

"Abi's father, the Premier, requested CIA help in tracking down Lei Han and his gang. I was recruited within hours of the shooting. Later, Abi figured out my role at the funeral and confronted me about it. Few people know my true identity because Lei Han remains a national security threat and I am still undercover. Even in Korea, I wanted to tell you, but could not out of fear—Forgive me."

Ruth looked into his eyes, stepped up, threw her arms around him, and kissed him.

Without a word, Ruth took his hand and he walked with her to the dorm. On the steps, she turned to kiss him again and went inside.

Luke stood for a few moments watching her go into the building then walked to his car.

Chapter 23

While Luke enjoyed a quiet weekend, on Saturday morning Tom's secure cell phone buzzed.

"Tom, this is Roscoe. Sorry to call you so early on a Saturday. Remember the toy factory that I told you about in Manchuria?"

"Sure. The one with the big titanium order?"

"That's the one. I just got satellite images showing that these guys made a big shipment late Friday night their time. Four separate eighteen wheelers loaded up and shipped out to different ports—one north through Russia, another east through North Korea, and the other two south to different Chinese ports."

"That can't be good. Is there any way to track those shipments?"

"Not really. The shipping containers used looked like they were painted black, but who can say? Each of them took a route through mountain tunnels and remained there until our satellite went out of range. They could have been repainted the containers or transferred their contents to other trucks."

"If they have manufactured receivers for pop-up mines, they may have shipped thousands, and we have no idea where to intercept them?"

"That's the current status."

"Anything else that you can tell me?"

"It may not be important, but the maximum depth of Heaven Lake is 1,260 feet—the average depth is half of that. That suggests that the maximum operational usefulness of the receivers is under that depth. If their researchers were lazy, the maximum depth would be no more than about six hundred feet."

"How does anchorage affect the mines' operational effectiveness?"

"Good point—these mines would need to be anchored for weeks, months, or even years. Otherwise, currents could wash them away from their intended sphere of operations. Because of that problem and the intense water pressures at such depths, my gut tells me to look for targets in water no more than about three hundred feet."

"Question—I know mines are usually designed to set and forget. What are the chances that they designed these receivers with a fail-safe capacity that we might hack into?"

"Slim to none. Fail-safe capacity substantially increases the complexity of the device, which increases the cost and lengthens the time required in design and testing. Unsophisticated mines are like a sucker punch. They only work when no one sees it coming, and don't have readily-available counter-measures."

"Roscoe—you are the man. I owe you a good steak dinner."

Chapter 24

Monday morning, Luke and Natalie met at five a.m. for the commute from McLean to Quantico to avoid the rush-hour traffic and have time to work out before classes began at eight. Like typical commuters, Luke drove and Natalie slept, having agreed that Natalie would drive on Fridays and let Luke sleep. Conversation only began after checking in and meeting at the gym for a good run.

"How was your weekend?" Luke asked.

"Pretty typical. Missed you at church," Natalie responded.

"I've taken a leave of absence for the next three months. Ruth's church invited me to preach."

"How did it go?"

"I seemed to connect with the group, but Ruth is behind in her schoolwork and experiencing grief over her dad's passing."

"Sounds challenging."

"Basically, it's hard to hang with grieving people."

"Did you get emotionally hijacked seeing her grief?"

"Come again?"

"Emotional hijacking occurs when someone else's issue triggers your own."

"Now that you mention it—after our parting yesterday, I sulked all afternoon in my own grief from losing my son and ex-wife, Sarah. Lotta water under the bridge in recent months."

"I noticed. You have held up pretty well for someone experiencing so much loss and having gone through so much danger and stress."

"Thanks for noticing. How do you know about this hijacking stuff?"

"I studied psychology and clinical counseling in college. I hope to become an FBI profiler."

"Yikes. No wonder you saw through my cover."

"It helped to know you and your son—the church is a family, right?"

Luke and Natalie ran on, not saying much.

Chapter 25

Monday morning, when Tom reported to work, Director Peters' assistant caught him walking up the stairs.

"Follow me," she said escorting him up to the director's office.

The director was waiting and shook Tom's hand as he led him into his office. "I have to brief the President within the hour on the Chinese situation. Give me a two-minute summary of what you have learned." The director opened his hand towards the couch, where they sat next to each other.

"Chinese and North Korean politics appear to be in motion—something we haven't seen in recent history."

"This is disturbing. How did you reach this conclusion?"

"In our last conversation, I asked permission to speak with my friend, Harry Bai, on the question of a leadership transition in the North Korean RGB."

"Yes. I remember."

"Harry was willing to answer the questions but could only share rumors about the removal of Director Parks. Furthermore, he was uninformed about the location of Lei Han, who had been in Chinese custody, but I observed him here in McLean personally only days ago. Both questions would normally fall in his bailiwick as Director of State Security."

"Absolutely."

"Because I've the upmost respect for Harry's competence and integrity, I can only conclude that he has been cut out of the loop—a very disturbing development because it suggests a powerful shift within the Chinese government."

"What else have you learned?"

"Director Parks, before he disappeared, shared that his mission in Cuba was to convince the Cubans to deploy pop-up mines in key U.S. harbors in advance of a Chinese invasion of Taiwan. This was an incredulous statement until I confirmed a design and testing site for the key component in the construction of these mines. Satellite imagery suggests that these components shipped from that site on Friday night."

"Ouch! Do we know where they are headed?"

"The shipment was broken up into four shipping containers that were headed for four separate ports of exit—Russia, North Korean, and two in China. Cuba is our only known prospective destination. Obviously, others are possible."

"Thank you. Let's go brief the President."

Director Peters' assistant guided the director and Tom to a limousine waiting in front of the building.

§

At the White House Monday morning briefing, the theme of the day was Taiwan and China. When the CIA's turn at bat came up, Director Peters gave a brief introduction, but then presented Tom and asked him to share his thoughts on recent developments. When Tom finished, the NSA director slid a photograph over the table to him.

"Does this device look like the receiver that you

described being shipped from Tianchi Toy?"

Tom turned the photograph around and examined it. "Where did you get this?"

"This photograph was intercepted from a passenger on a flight from Vladivostok to Beirut, Lebanon, last night."

"The timeline is consistent with the shipments from Tianchi Toy to Russia observed on Friday night, but just barely."

"Someone is in a hurry," The NSA director observed.

"This photograph gives the impression that this device was manufactured to look like a cell phone, but it has no screen, only buttons. It could be a receiver for a pop-up mine. Did we get physical possession of this device?"

"No. The image was picked up from an airport security screening camera electronically. Our analyst's artificial intelligence program kicked it out immediately as not matching any known device, but even on close examination of the photo, she had no idea what to make of it."

"Good catch. We have to assume that we have confirmation of a receiver shipment to Beirut. Naval intelligence needs to see this."

"Right. We're on it."

"Because we know that potentially thousands of these devices were manufactured, this airport catch must be a mere sample being shared with potential collaborators."

§

During the limo ride back to Langley, Director Peters and Tom reviewed the morning's discussion.

"It looks like we have an emerging problem with these receiver shipments," the director began.

"Clearly. If we can intercept these shipments, we can sandbag this entire strategy, but how do we begin?" Tom opined.

"I think that we have to start with Director Parks' original disclosure—Cuba is our best clue as to what's happening here. Whom do we have in Havana?"

"Effectively no one. Havana has been a sleepy

post since the embassy was reopened. Their main business function has been approving tourist visas."

"That needs to change. We need to see if we can find Director Parks and quietly keep an eye on possible receiver shipments and pop-up mine assembly and seeding."

"Luke Stevens has met Director Parks. He could also use a safe place to begin his on-the-job training as an operative."

"I'm not sure that Havana is a safe posting at this point. Isn't he still going through training at Quantico?"

"Field training is mostly on-the-job stuff. Quantico training is more helpful getting comfortable working with other agents stateside."

"Havana is a priority. Pull Stevens out of Quantico and get him ready to travel. Because he is more of an analyst, you may need to team him up with a seasoned agent."

Chapter 26

Monday, Tom texted Ruth asking for her to call him.

"Hello, Tom? This is Ruth. I'm between classes. You asked me to call," Ruth said, fast walking to class.

"To follow up on our last conversation, I would like to find Director Parks, assuming he is alive and in hiding. How would I go about finding him?"

"Did you try to call him on the number that he gave you?"

"Actually, no. It sounds obvious to call, but only this morning did I have a need."

"Call him. He likely kept that phone, but even secure lines in North Korea are not necessarily private. Use it but be brief. If he does not answer, text that number with a secure way for him to reach you."

"That's helpful advice."

"Got to go." Ruth walked into class and sat down.

§

After hanging up the phone with Ruth, Tom called Roscoe Billings.

"Hello, Roscoe? Are you going to be around the office for the next couple hours?"

"Yes. I assume that you want to follow up on the White House briefing earlier this morning."

"Word travels fast. See you in about forty-five minutes."

"I'll be here."

Tom borrowed a car and driver from the motor pool and headed over to the model basin. Roscoe's office door was open and Tom walked in.

"Tom, we're going to have to stop meeting like this. What's on your mind?"

"I need to pull together a small team to take the point in Havana, Cuba, to smoke out these pop-up mines, and I need a team leader. Are you interested?

"Cuba's beautiful this time of year, but aren't you worried about my age? I hit seventy this year. Most of my colleagues and former team members retired years ago."

"Age is not a factor. I need someone who's experienced and won't hit the fire alarm unnecessarily. This project has too much visibility."

"Whom will I be working with?"

"Your cover story is that this is a training mission. You are breaking in a new field operative in a low-profile, sleepy embassy. Even the ambassador will not be read in. You will report directly to me."

"Sounds like vacation with pay. When do I start?"

"Hopefully, in the morning. I need to collect your assistant."

"Do I know him?"

"Do you still teach at the FBI Academy?"

"Yes. I was there on Tuesday."

"Luke Stevens was one of your students last week."

"I saw his name on the roster."

"I should be able to pull him out of class today, so plan to report to Langley in the morning for orientation for field operatives."

"Sounds like a plan. What time?"

"I'm usually here at eight."

§

Tom returned to his car and headed back to Langley. On the way, he called Roger Smith, director of the FBI Academy.

"Hello, Roger? This is Tom Roberts."

"So you need me to pull Luke Stevens out of class?"

"Have him call me ASAP and report to Langley at eight o'clock tomorrow morning."

"He's not going to finish the program here, is he?"

"No. He is going into orientation for a field assignment. Tell him to bring his FBI uniform and swag with him."

"No problem. We sport some of the world's most famous drop-outs."

Thirty minutes later, Luke called Tom and reported that he was on his way up Interstate 95 traveling towards McLean.

§

Tom topped off a long day with a trip down to the Latin America and Caribbean branch. The branch chief, Ana Maria Santos Fuentes, who preferred to be known as Flaca, looked up as he came in the door.

"I wondered how long it would take you to pay me a visit."

"Flaca, we have to stop meeting like this, people will talk."

"Let's give them something to talk about. You have been avoiding me."

"My wife curses, taking your name in vain. There's a reason I hide in my office."

"Dios mío. Trabajo demasiado y me acusan de divertirme demasiado," Flaca responded.

"Poor baby. You work too much and still stand accused of having too much fun? Maybe it's because you clean up too nicely."

"That must be it. Tell me about this Havana assignment you are planning."

"How do you know about that? I haven't even briefed my team."

"You talk too much in front of your Puerto Rican driver."

"No confidence is confidential. Still, I need to read you in because I need your help."

"Let's go into my office." Flaca walked into her office, waved an invitation to sit at a small table, and closed the door. "*¿Qué hay?*"

"Through their North Korean counterparts, the Chinese are trying to convince the Cubans to mine U.S. harbors to stifle the response to an invasion of Taiwan. We learned over the weekend that the key component to these mines has been manufactured and shipped from four ports across East Asia."

"This has been confirmed?"

"Yes. A photograph of one of these components was intercepted yesterday in Beirut. My question to you is why would the Cubans risk alienating the United States after so many years of progress in our relations?"

"Hmm. Good question. I can think of some petty reasons—historical resentments, the intelligence service embarrassment last fall, general ambitions, but they don't add up to a serious military engagement, even a surreptitious one. The Cubans have been more interested in firing up the tourist trade in recent years. They have even begun quietly helping us interdict drug shipments."

"What might change their minds?"

"I would monitor financial flows to see if serious payments are being offered or if some serious blackmail was involved. Cuban funny business usually shows up in different transfer pricing schemes."

"Transfer pricing?"

"Sure. A export shipment of coffee, sugar, or fruit will suddenly be priced at ten or even a hundred times the normal market price in international trade. Unless you are familiar with the markets involved, such transfer pricing would never be noticed. It's subtle, not like throwing a batch of diamonds in bottles of tequila—rock candy, which sometimes shows up in imports."

"I see. Do you normally monitor transfer prices?"

"No. Such analysis requires subject-matter experts that are in short supply. We only monitor transfer prices in response to a tip."

"Thanks for the head's up. This is helpful background for our Havana team. Are you available tomorrow to join in our field operative orientation?"

"Just let me know when and where. I'll clear my calendar."

Chapter 27

After speaking with Tom, Luke drove home, put away his FBI gear, and ate some dinner. Thinking ahead, he texted Natalie and called her mother to let her know he won't be able to drive Natalie home on Friday evening. Not knowing what else to do, he put on his running outfit and went for a jog. *What will I tell Ruth? How will she react?* When he arrived home, he decided to call her.

"Hello, Ruth?"

"Hey, Luke. What's up?"

"Sorry to bother you on a school night. I'm not sure about the details at this point, but I'm being assigned to work in the U.S. Embassy in Havana, Cuba, for the foreseeable future."

"Really, when?"

"Soon as I can get through orientation for field operatives—perhaps this week."

"That sounds like a hurry-up thing."

"Basically. I don't know much more about it, but I don't want our relationship to fall through the cracks."

"Okay. What do you propose?"

"If possible, we should get together before I go. Otherwise, make sure you leave Christmas open to come to Havana."

"It's March. Christmas is a long way off. Can I ask a question?"

"Of course."

"Is Natalie going to be in Havana?"

"Natalie? Why would Natalie go to Havana?"

"You tell me."

"I've no idea. I don't even know at this point with whom I'll be working."

"Of course not."

"Ruth, what is going on here?"

"I need to go." Ruth hung up.

Luke called her back, but she did not pick up. *Hmm. Seems I need to give Ruth a time-out and let her sort things out for herself.*

ACT FOUR

Chapter 28

Tuesday morning, Luke checked into his office at Langley. At quarter to eight, he wandered over to Tom's office to find Roscoe and Tom shooting the breeze.

"I hope that you have some strong coffee this morning. I'm not sure that I can sit through a lot of meetings without caffeination," Luke said.

"Don't worry about orientation, Ana Marie will get your attention," Tom responded.

"Ana Marie?"

"She is the branch chief for the Latin American and Caribbean Branch. She calls herself Flaca, which translates as skinny in Spanish but really means hotty," Tom explained.

"Seriously?" Luke looked at the ceiling.

"You can just call her Ms. Fluentes, if you like," Tom teased.

"Where are we meeting?" Luke asked.

"Follow me." Tom led them down the hall to a conference room where Flaca was setting up her laptop and projector.

Tom motioned for Luke and Roscoe to have a seat. "This morning, Ms. Fluentes will brief you on background pertaining to the U.S. Embassy in Havana, the Cuban relationship with the United States, and life in Cuba. At noon, we'll make a field trip for lunch to a local Cuban restaurant. Might I recommend ordering a *cubano* with *tostones*?"

"In Cuba, people are serious about lunch!" Flaca said.

"This afternoon, we'll go over details of the mission. Tomorrow, you leave for Havana at six a.m. out of Dulles, so schedules are tight. Questions?" Tom looked at Luke and Roscoe.

Luke glanced at Flaca and Roscoe.

"Joking aside, this project started yesterday with a White House briefing. Make no mistake, eyes are on this project," Tom observed.

§

Flaca turned her laptop on and stood. "Roscoe can brief Luke on policies, procedures, and protocols.

Let's start by defining the problem.""

Tom nodded. "Good point."

"In a formal sense, the Cuban revolution is over and the government is moving towards an open relationship with the United States, but the Cuban intelligence community has become the center of a dark, underground, counter-cultural mess. We normally think of computer hackers in Eastern Europe and Asian backwater countries, like North Korea, but Cuba is better positioned and connected to the Narco traffickers, drug gangs, and undocumented workers that flood America. Cuban intelligence officers get trained on the island, and then just melt into the woodwork in this hemisphere. They speak the language and are ethically, racially invisible in the American melting pot."

"We're not on holiday here anymore," Tom observed. "This is more insidious, more real."

"The old ideology was liberation theology. Today, the more dangerous ideology is cultural Marxism." Flaca said.

"Huh?" Roscoe asked.

"Where liberation theology mixed Christianity and Marxism, cultural Marxism mixes Marxism with gender. Instead of a political revolution, which flamed out with the fall of the Berlin Wall, we're talking cultural revolution—lionizing outsiders to disenfranchise insiders. When everyone is unhappy and bickering, drugged up and sexed up, nothing gets done. The revolution then can happen because no one is minding the store." Flaca continued.

"So the reason that the North Korea intelligence service came to Cuba was to jump on this bandwagon?" Tom asked.

"No. The North Koreans want to tap into some of these informal networks to fly under the radar. The drug cartels are experts at avoiding the U.S. Navy and Coast Guard, and they know the waters around U.S. ports. Seeding pop-up mines would be an easy job for such groups. In principle, they could even assemble the mines in the U.S. and seed them on the return trip from a drug run."

"Don't cocaine mother ships and submarines

drop their shipments on the ocean floor for later pick-up?" Roscoe exclaimed.

"Hey, you may be onto something, but they typically avoid detection by staying clear of shipping lanes," Tom observed.

"Sure, if they are the conduit for laying these mines, then the flag would be a change in their usual areas of operation," Flaca said.

"Good insight. I wonder if the Drug Enforcement Agency (DEA) tracks these ships and subs. I'll bet that at a minimum they could map out prior interdiction locations," Roscoe noted.

"Right. Any change in venue would be a flag for mining activity," Tom said.

"I hate to be the one to throw cold water on this discussion, but why would the cartels want to draw attention to themselves? Wouldn't it be bad for business? I doubt many of them are ideologically motivated, and too many hands would be involved to keep it a secret very long," Luke said.

"What I'm doing here is trying to widen the

scope of our thinking. We don't know the plan envisioned, but we'll miss it if we're narrow-minded and underestimate our adversaries," Flaca explained. "Think of them as smart, devious, and experienced at avoiding detection."

"And potentially evil," Tom said. "This is a good way to orient our thinking. Having said that, I think we have some actionable hypotheses to work with. Flaca—check with your DEA contacts about the location of previous interdictions. Roscoe—check with your friends at Naval Intelligence to identify what locations are the highest priority to keep clear of mines. Luke—let's walk down to the communications office to make sure everyone knows you and briefs you on protocols."

"Don't forget to circle back for lunch at eleven thirty. You don't want to miss the *cubanos* and *tostones,*" Flaca said with a smile.

Chapter 29

Ruth's eight o'clock class finished at ten-thirty. As she left the class building and started down the street towards her dorm, a taxi cab pulled up beside her and rolled down its window.

"You called for a cab?" Ruth looked to see Director Parks driving the cab.

"Yes. Of course." Ruth opened the cab door and got in.

"Your boyfriend, Luke, has been targeted for assassination," Director Parks told her.

"Luke? Why?"

"The new administration believes that he embarrassed North Korea both by escaping into China and by breaking up with Abi Ling." Director Parks drove around Georgetown aimlessly.

"Am I targeted too? I too helped him escape, and Abi Ling broke up with him because of me."

"And I helped him escape too, don't forget."

"Is that why Lei Han replaced you as RGB director?"

"No. No. These are all excuses. The reason for my replacement is that I was too open to normalizing relations with the West. Your boyfriend is the symbol of that evolving relationship."

"Why am I so lucky to be spared punishment?"

"Our Supreme Leader likes you and the fact that you have become the symbol of a young, successful, and fashionable North Korean woman."

"Mr. Director, how may I help you?"

"Warn Tom that Luke is being targeted."

"Tom asked me this past week how to get in touch with you."

"What did you tell him?"

"I told him that you may still answer your phone."

"That number is not safe." Director Parks handed Ruth a cell phone. "This phone is secure—give it to Tom."

"No problem."

Director Parks drove Ruth to her dormitory and dropped her off.

§

Ruth climbed the steps in her dormitory to the top floor where she could keep an eye on everyone that might approach her. Then she took out her phone and called Tom.

"Hello, Tom? Sorry to bother you during the workday. I just spoke with Director Parks and he gave me a secure phone to pass to you."

"Director Parks is in DC?"

"Yes. He warned me that Luke has been targeted for assassination. Is Luke okay?"

"Yes. He has been here with me all morning."

"Oh, great. I was so worried."

"Don't tell him, but I have had an FBI protection team watching him, even down at school."

"Really? At school?"

"Yes. You probably know one of the agents—have you met Natalie?"

"Natalie's part of his protection detail? Isn't she a bit young?"

"Natalie is the FBI's youngest agent and really

good at what she does."

"I would never have guessed."

"That's one of the reasons that she is so effective—no one would guess."

"I need to call Luke. What time does he get off work?"

"He should be home by six this evening. Tomorrow, his team flies to Havana so he needs to pack and get a good night's rest. While I have you on the phone, may I stop by your dorm this evening at eight to pick up the director's phone?"

"Sure. See you then."

§

Ruth called her uncle, Pastor Chǔ.

"Uncle, this is Ruth."

"Yes, Ruth. How are you? You don't usually call me during the day."

"I'm fine. I have a theological question."

"Sure. What is it?"

"I'm confused. Why do Christians here get so excited about Christmas? Is it just about Santa Claus,

Christmas trees, and getting gifts?"

"Oh, goodness no. Yes, there is a lot of commercialization of the holiday, but Christmas is much more than that."

"More?"

"Christmas is a holiday devoted to the joy of salvation. Easter is more reflective, focusing on the crucifixion and resurrection. Christmas is about the realization that God has not forgotten us and broke into our world to break the seductive power of sin and oppressive presence of darkness. You can be happy about receiving physical gifts, but the gift of salvation brings a much deeper joy. Nothing else can compare. Jesus is the light of the world, as the Apostle John put it."

"I see. How come Koreans aren't into Christmas like Americans?"

"That's one of those mysteries of life."

§

After dinner Tuesday evening, Ruth called Luke.

"I want to apologize for being so difficult the

last time we spoke, and I have changed my mind about Havana. I would love to come to Havana for Christmas."

"Happy to hear it. I fly to Havana in the morning. Our next conversation will be long distance."

"No problem. The time will pass quickly. Classes keep me fully occupied."

"Listen, I need to go and pack for my flight."

"So soon? Can't someone else save the world for a while?"

"I guess it's my turn."

"Text me when you board the plane and when you arrive."

"I'll do my best. I'm not sure about the reception in Cuba."

"Good point. It's another of those workers' paradises."

Chapter 30

At quarter to eight Tuesday evening, Tom walked from the Metro to Ruth's dorm. When he got in front of the building, a taxi pulled up alongside of him and rolled down the window.

"Tom, do have a minute?" Director Parks asked.

"For you, absolutely." Tom opened the cab door and got in.

"Sorry for the surprise visit. I have to be careful about revealing my location."

"I understand. Tell me what happened."

"Lei Han's allies have taken power in Beijing, and they specifically directed our Supreme Leader to remove me and install him."

"Why you?"

"China likes to use the RGB to do its dirty work. It gives them greater latitude in taking risks and more deniability. What is different this time is that China is asking North Korea to go to war with the United States. When I expressed apprehension privately, they moved to replace me."

"Do you think that China would relent on invading Taiwan if this pop-up mine initiative can be checked?"

"Yes. China realizes that it can only defeat Taiwan by cutting off its resupply because in the event of war, prepositioned munitions will be exhausted within weeks. Thus, the U.S. Navy plays a critical role in stopping a successful invasion. I proposed our meeting, hoping to avert this crisis by undermining its execution."

"How does this assassination plot against Luke Stevens fit into this plan?"

"It doesn't. My guess is that Lei Han is seeking revenge for his bruised ego."

"What about the Cubans?"

"The Cubans are not interested in helping with the pop-up mine initiative, but the Cuban intelligence service has a lot of agents who have wandered off the plantation, gotten wealthy from the drug trade, and operate independently of Havana. These were the people waiting for me in Havana. Lei Han knows these people well because of his contacts in the Triad opium trade. "

"So we're dealing with narco traffickers, not Cuban intelligence?"

"There is some overlap, but that's a fair characterization."

"Director Parks, how may I help you?"

"Call me on the phone that I left with Ruth if I can assist you. I cannot be seen working with you, but we share a common interest in preventing this war."

"Understood. I'll be discrete."

Director Parks dropped Tom off again in front of Ruth's dormitory. Tom climbed the stairs to her room. He knocked on her door, she answered and handed him the phone. Tom thanked her and left. As he exited the building, Tom heard an explosion about a block off.

In the morning, he learned that Director Parks' cab had been blown up and the body discovered inside burned beyond recognition.

§

Wednesday morning, Tom picked up Ruth and

drove to Dulles International Airport. He arranged with TSA to have Luke and Roscoe flagged down in security screening and join them in a conference room.

"Luke, Roscoe, your trip to Havana has been postponed until Friday," Tom explained.

Ruth ran over and threw her arms around Luke.

"Why?"

"Inspectors found a pressure bomb planted on your flight."

"Lei Han again?" Luke asked.

"Yes. Pressure bombs are his signature hit," Tom responded. "Until we deal with the Lei Han threat, you and Roscoe will be working for a couple days from a local safe house."

"What's special about Lei Han?" Luke asked.

"Lei Han is now the RGB Director, and he put out an assassination order on you. To cover up our discovery of the bomb, we'll delay the flight, claiming mechanical problems, send the passengers on an alternative flight, and put out fake news that the plane exploded over the Atlantic. You and Roscoe will be listed among those dead and lost at sea. The rest of the casualties will be bogus passengers."

"What about Havana?" Luke asked.

"I need to make a call to my contact in Havana. If things work out, you two will fly quietly out of Miami to Havana on Friday."

"Thanks, Tom. It's good to know that you've got our backs," Roscoe said.

§

Tom dropped Ruth off at school and then returned to his office at Langley. He immediately reported to Director Peters. Peters was in the middle of a staff meeting, but when he saw Tom come in, he dismissed everyone and ushered Tom into his office.

"You heard about the explosion downtown last night?" Director Peters asked.

"Yes. I was there. Do you want to be read in?"

"No details, just high-level sketch. The attempted airline bombing suggests that we may have a leak."

"It was a North Korean hit on a source of mine."

"Does it have implications for the Chinese

threat?"

"Yes. Changing of the guard stuff. North Korea is working with narco traffickers to seed the pop-up mines."

"Not the Cubans?"

"No. Cuban intelligence does, however, need to clean house. I need your permission to assist them with that task."

"Absolutely—send me an email to confirm the request and my approval. BTW, I heard that there was problem at Dulles airport this morning—what's that about?"

"Lei Han tried to take out our team with a pressure bomb on their flight to Havana. My source clued me into the threat, we found and defused the bomb—you probably saw the fake news report that we issued. Our team is holed up in a safe house here in Northern Virginia until Friday."

Director Peters nodded. "You might like to know that the FBI coroner issued a preliminary autopsy report this morning on the cab driver."

"What did he learn?"

"The remains were burned beyond recognition. The coroner could not identify the remains, but said that it was a man in his thirties riddled with bullet holes. The preliminary cause of death is gunshot wounds, not burning."

"That's not my source, although it was obviously his cab. Could you ask the FBI to put the release of the autopsy on the slow-mo?"

"No problem. We owe your source at least that much."

Tom returned to his office. He typed up an email to the director requesting permission to talk with JR Castro, chief to the Intelligence Directorate. Minutes later he received an approval email from Director Peters.

§

Tom walked down to Flaca's office.

"Flaca, sorry to barge in. I need to talk with your buddy, JR Castro. I thought that you should sit in."

"*Jefe JR* is not my buddy. He is just effusive when

it suits his purposes, like all good *Cubanos.*"

"Sure, but you're not Puerto Rican. Cubans seem to have a superiority complex relative to other Caribbeans."

"Okay, let me call him and I'll hand the call off to you."

"That works."

Flaca picked up a secure phone and dialed the number for the *Dirección de Inteligencia.*

"Buenos días, Dirección de Inteligencia. ¿Quién quiere?" A secretary asked.

"Hola, estoy buscando al Jefe, JR. Dile que llama el Flaco de la CIA." Flaca responded.

"No problem, Flaca. I'll put you through." A couple minutes pass.

"Flaca, how have you been? When are you going to come visit us?" JR asked.

"Actually, we're sending a team down this week. Tom will explain."

"Chief JR, how have you been?" Tom asked.

"We're enjoying the warm weather. How about

you?" JR responded.

"Northern Virginia has been rather dark and cold of late, so we thought that we would send some of our people down to help you enjoy the weather."

"Tell me more."

"What do you know about the North Koreans efforts to mine U.S. harbors?"

"The pop-up mines? We have nothing to do with that."

"So you do know. We propose to send a small team to Havana to gather information and, hopefully, to coordinate with you in cleaning up this mess. Can we count on your support?"

"I'll need to make inquiries. When is your team coming?"

"The plan is to send two agents on Friday to work at the U.S. Embassy."

"Okay. Let me get back to you tomorrow. Does this team have anything to do with the fake news report about a plane bombing yesterday?"

"The real attack was thwarted, so we threw up-smoke to cover our retreat."

"I hope everyone is okay."

"Thanks. Everyone is a bit on edge at the moment."

"Understandable. I'll try to let you know tomorrow whether we can work together more closely."

"Thanks again. *Hasta mañana.*"

"*Ciao.*"

Chapter 31

Thursday morning Tom received a call from Ruth.

"Good morning, Tom. How do I get in touch with Luke? I would like to see him before he leaves tomorrow."

"Security makes your request difficult. Luke is officially dead at the moment—we can't have people seeing him drive around Northern Virginia and even I don't know all the locations of our safe houses. How about I have him call you this afternoon for a video chat?"

"Okay. I understand. What time? I have class until three p.m."

"Alright. Let's shoot for four o'clock."

"Thanks, Tom."

§

Just after noon, Tom got a call from Chief JR.

"How are things in Langley?"

"We seem busy for some reason. What was the response to our proposal for a joint project?"

"We got a green light to work together, but we

want to keep a low profile and maintain our bad-boy image."

"Roger that. How would you like to proceed?"

"To keep things simple, we'll set up a room in the Hotel Nacional de Cuba, which is within walking distance from the U.S. Embassy, where our people can assist your agents. My office will drop off a secure phone and hotel details at the U.S. Embassy this afternoon to coordinate these arrangements."

"This afternoon?"

"My people tell me that your agents arrived in Havana about an hour ago."

"Interesting—your team is most efficient. Here in Langley, people think our team flies out tomorrow morning."

"We're good at what we do. The little fiasco with the gas gauge last fall was an embarrassment that we do not intend to repeat."

"Ah hah. Thank you for your help. What can we do for you?"

"We're looking for closer ties, not just a deal

now and then."

"Good. Talk with you soon."

Chapter 32

At four p.m., Ruth received an invitation to video connect through email. She clicked on the link and there was Luke.

"Ruth, how are you doing?"

"I just finished classes for the day." She heard a knock on her door. "Excuse me a minute, someone is at my door."

Ruth answered the door to find a delivery man, who handed her a package and asked her to sign for it. Ruth signed and he left. Ruth returned to her laptop with the package in hand. "I wasn't expecting anything."

"Open it."

Ruth opened the package to find a jewelry case. Inside was an engagement ring.

"What is this?" Ruth asked.

"Ruth, will you marry me?" Luke asked.

"Are you serious?"

"Very, please marry me."

"You are crazy, but—Yes. I would love to spend my life with you." Ruth put on the engagement ring and held it up to the screen.

"I know this is very sudden, but the attempted bombing the other day helped clarify my priorities. I love you and do not want to lose you. So you know, I arrived this morning in Havana a bit ahead of schedule."

"Havana, Cuba?"

"Yes. Because of security concerns, we moved up our flight."

"Thank you for the ring. Let's talk Sunday afternoon about plans. Between now and then, I'll talk to my mom."

"Absolutely. Talk to you Sunday."

"Love you."

"Love you."

Chapter 33

After finishing his talk with Ruth, Luke received a secure phone via courier at his office in the U.S. Embassy. He walked down to Roscoes' office.

"What do you make of our new relationship with the *Dirección de Inteligencia* (DI)?" Luke asked.

"Tom sent us both an email saying we have a green light to coordinate with DI via this secure phone that you received. He also said to keep conversations short and to the point. Don't share more information than is pertinent to the task at hand," Roscoe said.

"Let's call them. The Hotel Nacional is within walking distance. Let's go over and check it out. I could use some exercise. Your Spanish is better than mine." Luke handed the phone to Roscoe, who dialed the hotel number.

"Hello, this is Roscoe Billings."

"Yes, Agent Billings."

"We're considering a walk over to the Hotel Nacional to scope out the arrangements. Are you ready for us?"

"Yes. Everything is in place. Go to the third floor, room 301. A team to assist you will be waiting."

"Okay. It's four-thirty. We should be there in fifteen minutes."

Chapter 34

Tom received a call over the secure phone that Director Parks gave him.

"Hello, Director Parks?"

"Yes. Tom."

"Thank goodness, you are okay."

"My wife frequently begs me to go into another line of work."

"I understand. What's up?"

"A little birdie told me that Lei Han is currently in Panama City looking for a black container bound for Cartagena, Columbia. Apparently, the container ship transporting this container off-loaded it at Panama City. The ship was too heavy to pass through the canal because of the drought and low water levels associated with the *El Niño* weather pattern this year. The choice of containers was entirely random—the black container just happened to be on top of the deck. This problem arose within the last twenty-four hours."

"What are the odds that this is the Chinese shipment of pop-up mine receivers?" Tom asked.

"The odds are good. Otherwise, why the special attention from Lei Han?"

"Wow."

"The story gets better. The only way across the Darién Gap between Panama and Columbia is via river ferry to Turbo, Columbia. There are no roads at all through this region. The ferry is a relic of another era, so a black container would stand out."

"Director Parks, this is serious intel. Thank you."

§

Tom called Roscoe.

"Hello, Roscoe? Where are you?

"Luke and I are walking over to the Hotel Nacional."

"I know that you and Luke have had a long day, but we have an emergency. Lei Han has been sighted in Panama City along with a black container, presumably of pop-up mine receivers, bound for Cartagena."

"How can I help?

"Ask the DI if they have people on the ground

in Cartagena, Columbia. If this shipment slips through our fingers in Panama City, it would be nice to have the Cubans waiting for them in Cartagena. We need the shipment and Lei Han both intact. A working receiver may offer clues on disabling it, and Lei Han can lead us to the other three shipping containers."

"Got it."

"Be polite, but dial back to the Embassy as soon as you can. I'll alert the Embassy staff that they are on call this evening. This is likely to be an all-nighter."

"I'll call if I learn anything," Roscoe said.

Chapter 35

Roscoe and Luke arrived at the *Hotel Nacional,* took the elevator to the third floor, and knocked on Room 301. A stunning, twenty-something woman in a white silk dress answered the door.

"Agents Billings and Stevens, please come in," she said.

They walked in the room to find Chief JR waiting for them.

"Welcome. My name is Castro, but please just call me JR." JR extended his hand to shake theirs. "Thank you for coming. I trust that you had a pleasant flight."

"Thank you. It's good to be here. I have always wanted to visit Havana," Luke said with a smile.

"How can we be of assistance?" JR asked.

"How much do you know about our pop-up mine concern?" Roscoe asked.

"The North Koreans approached us about importing mine receivers and assembling the mines here in Cuba, but we refused. No technical details were shared with us," JR confided.

"Thank you for being frank. We have just received word that a shipment of receivers got offloaded from a container ship at Panama City and are being transported to Cartagena, Columbia. Lei Han, the new director of RGB in North Korea has flown in to supervise this shipment. We hope to intercept them before they reach Cartagena. We have been asked to see if you have people in place in Cartagena who might detain them if our efforts fail," Roscoe said.

"Detain them?" JR inquired.

"We need Lei Han alive to question him about the other shipments and we would like to examine one of these receivers to analyze how they might be compromised or disabled remotely. Who knows how many of these pop-up mines have already been deployed?" Roscoe explained.

"Clearly. If Lei Han is accompanying this shipment, then chances are good that he has a security team with him and will resist efforts to detain him," JR observed.

"You are no doubt correct about that," Roscoe replied.

"I'll make inquiries about your request. Meanwhile, I suspect that you will want to return to the Embassy," JR said.

"Yes. Any help that you can offer with this operation would be most appreciated," Roscoe said, standing to leave.

"The evening is upon us. Let's touch base at nine tomorrow morning," JR suggested.

"Very good. Thank you for your support. It's most encouraging. I have your phone."

Roscoe and Luke left the hotel and walked back to the embassy. On the way, Roscoe called Tom to report on his conversation with Chief JR.

§

After Roscoe hung up the phone, Tom called his NSA contact.

"I need an intercept on a secure phone call from Havana to Panama or Columbia in the last fifteen minutes ongoing." Tom asked.

"One minute," The operator responded.

Tom took a bite from his dinner.

"You are in luck. In the past hour, there has only been one phone call. Do you want a transcript?"

"Yes. I need a transcript and the geo-position of the callers."

"The Havana call came from the *Hotel Nacional.* The call on the other end was Panama City."

"Good. Read me the transcript."

The operator read:

JR: *Hello, Lei Han? They are on to you.*

Lei Han: *JR, do they know the location of the San Diego, San Francisco, and Honolulu shipments?*

JR: *No. They are only aware of the container in Panama.*

Lei Han: *Okay, thanks. Talk to you later.*

JR: *Ciaco.*

"That's it. They hung up."

"You are a life saver. Send me the transcript and locations via email," Tom said.

"Roger that. Happy to help."

§

Armed with intel from NSA, Tom called CIA operations.

"Whom do we have in Panama City?" he asked.

"We have a team of a dozen special agents who work closely with the DEA and the Canal Authority," the night officer responded.

"I'm sending you coordinates for a pickup. The target is a North Korean named Lei Han. He is likely to have a security team with him," Tom said.

"I got the coordinates. They correspond to a hotel."

"I need this guy alive. How soon can the team be mobilized?"

"We can pick him up at four a.m. local time."

"That works. How soon can you have eyes on the hotel?"

"Almost immediately. That hotel is across the street from the DEA office in Panama City."

"Good. Good. Lei Han is babysitting a black

container with a shipment of weapons—we need to locate and seize that container."

"We'll do our best."

"Thanks. I need this guy on a military transport to Gitmo on the QT ASAP. If and when you get an example of this weapon, I need it air freighted to Langley."

"Understood."

Lei Han came into custody without incident on Friday at 4 a.m. He had an example of the pop-up mine receiver in his possession, which was shipped to Langley Friday afternoon. Tom recalled Roscoe and Luke to Langley, and they left Havana quietly on a Saturday morning flight.

Chapter 36

Sunday morning Luke walked into the university cafeteria just in time to surprise Ruth and take part in the Korean Alliance worship service.

"Luke, I thought that you were in Havana," Ruth exclaimed.

"Not anymore."

"You're back permanently?"

"Sorry to disappoint. I was hoping for a Havana wedding at Christmas, but a McLean wedding will have to do."

"McLean is better. My mom is afraid to travel to Cuba."

"Smart mom."

ABOUT

Author Stephen W. Hiemstra lives in Centreville, Virginia with Maryam, his wife of more than thirty-five years. They have three grown children.

Stephen worked as an economist for twenty-seven years in more than five federal agencies, where he published numerous government studies, magazine articles, and book reviews. Check WorldCat.org for a complete listing of volumes available in a library near you.

Stephen has published a six-book, Christian spirituality series. He wrote his first book, *A Christian Guide to Spirituality* in 2014. In 2016, he wrote a second book, *Life in Tension*. In 2017, he published a memoir, *Called Along the Way*. In 2019, he published *Simple Faith*. In 2020, he published *Living in Christ*. His sixth book—*Image and Illumination*—was published in 2023.

He began a new Image of God series with the publication of *Image of God in the Parables* (2023) and *Image of the Holy Spirit and the Church* (2023).

Two books from his Christian spirituality series are

available in Spanish: *Una Guía Cristiana a la Espiritualidad* (2015) and *Vida en Tensión* (2021). He also published his first book in German: *Ein Christlicher Leitfaden zur Spiritualität* (2022).

In 2021, he published his debut novella, *Masquerade*, and rewrote it as a screenplay under the title: *Brandishing the Blue*. In 2023, he published a sequel, *The Detour*, and adapted it as a screenplay by the same name.

Stephen published his first hardcover book, *Everyday Prayers for Everyday People* (2018). He also published an ebook compilation book, *Spiritual Trilogy*, that year.

Stephen has a Masters of Divinity (MDiv, 2013) from Gordon-Conwell Theological Seminary in Charlotte, North Carolina. His doctorate (Ph.D., 1985) is in agricultural economics from Michigan State University. He studied in Puerto Rico and in Germany, and speaks Spanish and German.

Correspond with Stephen at T2Pneuma@gmail.com or follow his blog at http://www.T2Pneuma.net.

If you enjoyed *Christmas in Havana*, please post a review online.